The Purchase of Order

Winner of
**THE FLANNERY O'CONNOR AWARD
FOR SHORT FICTION**

The Purchase
of Order

Stories by Gail Galloway Adams

The University of Georgia Press

Athens and London

© 1988 by Gail Galloway Adams
Published by the University of Georgia Press
Athens, Georgia 30602
All rights reserved
Set in Bookman
The paper in this book meets the guidelines for
permanence and durability of the Committee on
Production Guidelines for Book Longevity of the
Council on Library Resources.

Printed in the United States of America

91 90 89 88   5 4 3 2 1

Library of Congress Cataloging in Publication Data

Adams, Gail Galloway.
The purchase of order.

Contents: Inside dope—Marva Jean Howard
confesses—Doing yoga—[etc.]
I. Title.
PS3551.D356P87 1988   813'.54   88-4724
ISBN 0-8203-1040-9 (alk. paper)

"Inside Dope" was first published in the North
American Review and was selected for inclusion in
Editor's Choice. "A Teller's Tale" originally appeared
in The Georgia Review.

Illustration by Jim Chapman

For my family

The publication of this book is supported by a grant from the National Endowment for the Arts, a federal agency.

Contents

The Purchase of Order

Inside Dope

This is a story about being in love with a man named Billy Lee Boaz, only he's called Bisher, don't ask me why. You need to know what he looks like because Bisher is a type, if men don't recognize, at least the women will.

First, a Boaz is not big. Five foot six is about as tall as they get, and they are dark with black hair and eyes, real tanned skin, and bodies just as trim and tight as their lips are wet and loose. They have bandits' faces, with bright shiny eyes that gleam in a dashboard's light, white teeth that do the same, and they are as good in bed as they are at working on the engine of a Pontiac. They don't do sports, except sometimes if the high school is small enough you'll see them on the football line digging in like baby buffalo; stamina and spite keep them there against all odds. They usually aim their every action to rewards, and the mean variety end up in the service yelling at shaved-head recruits and being fussy over lockers. The civilian ones are good-natured boys, then men, who smile a lot. They are the kind who, when they come down to breakfast in clean white T-shirts and starched khaki pants, freshly showered and shaved, come smiling into the kitchen. Their hair is always cut the same, "some off the back and sides, just barely trim the top," and around each ear is pared an arch the color of their palms, their soles, and underneath their underwear.

They're jittery men too, jiggling change as they stand, walking forward lightly on their toes, slumping back hard into their heels, and somehow you are always aware of them from the navel down. Although they do nothing with their hands and arms to indicate their lower parts, still, the itch of lust is in the air. When they love you they are given to coming up and getting push-up placed with you against the wall; then they lean down to lick your throat. Before you gasp they unroll a pack of Luckies tucked like a second bicep in their shirt, and light one in a dramatic way: scratching the match against their thigh, snapping it in two with a nail, or deliberately letting the flame burn into their fingerpads. They are also the kind of men who groan when it feels good, and Bisher, who was my brother-in-law, had all these qualities.

But of course, finally, Bisher is different and that's why I'm telling about him. Bisher was, and is, a genius. Everyone attests to that, even the principal who threw him out of school. Bisher works (where he has for years) at the Standard Shell station and wears a blue blouse with his name embroidered on his chest, an oval with a red satin stitch of *Boaz, Bill* right over his heart. He's the one who taught me to call a work shirt a blouse. "More uniform," he grinned, explaining that in the Army they call them blouses instead of shirts and "no one ever called dogfaces feminine." Then he folded in the sides of cloth like wrappings on a gift and tucked them in his pants. That was the summer I was fifteen, and I sat on the shag rug listening to, watching, and admiring Bisher.

My sister Ellen married Bisher at the end of her junior year in high school, and there's no need to go into what that did to our family. First, everyone almost died; then they cried from March to June, and finally, when my parents realized those two would not give up, they were wed under my father's guiding prayers, and we all gave thanks that one of the two—probably Bisher— had the sense to hold off babies for a while. In towns like ours, as soon as a marriage was announced, countdown began. People bought layettes the same day they bought a plate for the bride's table setting.

After a return from a honeymoon in "Gay Mehico," Ellen and

3
Inside Dope

Bisher made our third floor home. The room had been ours—mine and Ellen's, I mean—and was really two rooms with a long hall in between, a sink curtained off at one end and a toilet in a closet near the stair. "Deluxe," Bisher said the day he moved in. "I'll add this to my list of ten best spots to stay from here to Amarillo." Ellen blushed to see him standing there amidst our pink stuffed bears and faded rag rugs. I moved reluctantly down to a room which was used once or twice a year for visiting missionaries, more often for making costumes for the church's plays. With Bisher upstairs, our lives took on new rhythms and new ways.

My dad did not, of course, like Bisher, but being a Christian thought he should, and tried to talk to his new son-in-law each day. "Well, young man . . ." Dad would clear his throat. "Well, Billy Lee."

"Call me Bisher, sir," said Bisher. So Daddy would nod and ask, "Have a good day?"

"Yes, sir," Bisher'd reply as snappy as an ensign in starched pants. Then he'd wink at me and purse his lips at Ellen, which made me giggle and her blush, then both snicker.

My mother always caught these three-way exchanges, saw us, her daughters, as traitors, and would draw her lips together and pale. She absolutely hated, detested, despised Billy Lee. She refused to call him Bisher, forbade our father to, cursed "that Boaz," his family, his pets, and malign chance that put him here in this town when he should have been in Houston getting mugged. "Just trash," she'd mutter, "nothing but trash. I never thought I'd raise my Ellen to marry trash."

I would sit on a high stool in the kitchen waiting for Mamma to finish washing the dishes I was to dry, and listen to her tirades against Bisher, and wonder why he made her feel that way. "It's lust, nothing but lust," she'd said once, then flushed, slapped me on the arm right where I was picking a scab off a mosquito bite, and yelled at me to get upstairs to my room and stop hanging around minding everybody's business, which I thought wasn't fair. But as I moped my way to the room beneath the bed where Ellen and Bisher slept, I knew then, as now, that no matter what my mother said, I was on my sister's side, and Bisher's. And I also knew that I would love that short dark boy until the day I died.

Bisher was able, finally and always, to get around my mother as he got around everyone. He won her over in the end, for all the time she was dying the one person she ever wanted to see was him. "Where is that scamp?" she'd ask. "He worries me to death." She'd pull at the collar of her bed jacket, push at her limp hair, and say, "I wouldn't care to see him again." The door'd creep open and Bisher's face would appear, dark and shiny as mischief. "Got a minute, madame?" he'd whisper, letting his eyes look shyly everywhere except at her until she'd say, "Come on in, you're letting air out to the hall." Then Bisher'd slip into the room so quick if you didn't know better you'd think he made his living as a second-story man, or maybe was a meter man gone bad and gone to bed with the lady of the house.

But like everybody else he touched, he touched our mother, made her do things she'd never dreamed of. He taught her to smoke on her deathbed. We could hear her gasp for breath and laugh between puffs and coughs. "Oh, Lord," she'd say, or pray, with stammering breath, "This is so wrong," and then peer closely at the end of her Camel to see if it would contradict. "Look here," Bisher'd command, and she'd watch him fill the room with smoky rings. She learned that too. It was disconcerting to creak open the door to check and see if she was resting well and catch her lying there, propped up on ruffled pillows, head tilted back to the ceiling, her mouth a perfect "O" as it puffed out those rings until they circled her like Saturn's do. Now I understand that that was one of Bisher's secrets. He's the kind of man who'll take you to a raunchy honky-tonk if you want to go, and all night

while you are sipping 3.2 beer his feet will be tapping yours under the table and he'll be winking at you or nudging you as if to
say, "Why aren't you bad?" He let you play it fast, but safe, and
you were grateful to him for it.

I wouldn't say that Bisher's what they call a good old boy. He's
not. At least, I don't think he is. For although he works on cars
and engines and loves them, he doesn't care for guns. He has
one, everybody does, but his hangs behind the door, forgotten as
a worn-out coat. "I never liked hunting much," he said one night
in the kitchen when we were helping Mamma skin rabbits a
church elder had brought. Dumped out of a gunny sack onto the
floor, the rabbits filled the room with their blood-splotched fur.
Ellen, pregnant with her first, ran to throw up; Mamma murmured, "Oh, Lord," and even Daddy, who preached of death as a
new beginning, looked distressed.

"Let's make them look like meat," Bisher said, "then they won't
trouble us as much." He heaped them in a plastic tub where they
hung limp as coronation trim to be sewed on, then took them to
the porch. After they were skinned and all the leavings but their
lucky feet buried, they bubbled pale and shimmering in a black
iron pot.

"No, I never cared for hunting," Bisher said thoughtfully when
all that had been done. "Because I always thought just before I
shot. . ." He paused, looked apologetically at my father. "What if
it's true we're born again, and in another body, say, like a deer?
Why, I couldn't shoot a deer to save my life, cause every time I'd
remember Lewis Moon and how he liked to run before he died.
Why, what if Lewis was that deer? Excuse me, sir."

My daddy muttered, "Quite all right," and hurried out to write
up a lesson for the Senior Sunday School with two main
themes—Number 1: Do we need to hunt our animal friends?
and Number 2: Beliefs on coming back to life that Christians
should put right on out of their heads.

But what made Bisher unique was that he was a genius, and

how he got to be one is legend in our town. Others have tried his trick since, just to end up laughingstocks when they have failed. There has been only one other acknowledged genius in this whole county, and George Shapland was never any fun like Bisher. He was always tucked up in a book, which Bisher said proved he wasn't a natural genius. "Not that there is a thing wrong with books. It's just that they don't have no place." George graduated from high school at age fifteen after having proved the geometry teacher wrong and having put the history teacher down (both were coaches, so shouldn't be blamed for being soft in hard subjects), and then he went to State Tech where he took a double load of everything and made friends with others like himself who cluttered up cafeteria tables with maps and measuring instruments. Later it was rumored he became a monk. But Bisher's genius wasn't like George's ordinary kind, for Bisher's brain was pure, and how he brought it to the attention of the authorities was genius enough.

A new teacher came to teach English and the Romance tongues, and one week into French, Bisher's genius was revealed. Called on to read a page of Lesson II, he balked at his desk, slumped into his heels, and said in French he'd rather not. The rest of the students didn't know what he said, thought it was filth and that that was why the teacher gasped and said, "You read it, you canard." When Bisher quacked and waddled to the front, the others didn't know what was going on. They now thought Bisher was making bathroom gestures, sounds. He jumped on the teacher's desk; then, barely looking at the text, he read Lesson II, skipped on to IV, ending up with number XII, and he answered all the questions too. The other students still thought he was Danny Kaye-ing them, making Frenchy sounds, making fun of French, so they were laughing at his ooo la la's, but meanwhile the teacher had caught on to Bisher's brain and stood there listening to him reel off syllables like de Gaulle.

Inside Dope

When Bisher finished a rundown of the hardest, longest words in the index, translating all of them, a silence fell upon the room. "Is he right?" whispered a semibright boy, and the teacher numbly nodded her head. When she did, Bisher, who was still standing on the desk, now holding the book across his chest in a Napoleon stance, suddenly, without a sideways glance, hurled that text out the window, splintering the glass. At the crash, he jumped to flee the room, the teacher in pursuit, screaming "My boy, my boy, my dear dear boy" in French.

Bisher got kicked out of school about ten minutes later, even though the teacher intervened, claiming (it was the first time) Bisher's genius. The principal would hear none of this. "Don't let me hear of this boy's genius. I call it fits myself. There's at least ten idiots in the institute can reel off dates and times better than this Billy Lee 'Bisher' Boaz boy. And as for this last—this French episode—why, I don't know." He shook his hands from the wrist as if that limpness signified Paris and all its decadence. Then he threw Bisher out, saying the reasons were breaking windows and the backs of books and disrespect for a foreign land.

Once expelled, Bisher was stripped not only of the lessons he already knew, but of all the offices he held, which, though many, were not various. He was the sergeant at arms for every club from Future Nurses to the Lindbergh Boys. He had more pictures in the *Cattle Call* annual than anybody but the Snowball Queen, but that year he was officially excised, and every organization picture had an oblong blank that once was Billy Lee. He signed those anyway with Greek signs.

The second reason he was a genius was inside dope. What that means is that Bisher knew something about everything—he really did. Like all smart men, he claimed to have read the dictionary from *A* to *Z*, and was always threatening to start in on the *Britannica*. In every conversation Bisher had things to add, and always they were interesting. He was like those columns in the newspaper called "Ask Mr. Tweedles" where people write in to ask "What are warts made of?" and "Why are tulips bulbs?" That is what Bisher Boaz could do too—not only explain warts in scientific terms, he could tell you about all the different kinds of warts, from plantars on your feet to venereal on your you-know-where. But, unlike a Tweedles, who had to stop at column's end, Bisher didn't. If you showed the slightest bit of interest, as I did, since my hands were always covered with warts—seed pearls of them ringing my fingers, grits of them on my fingertips—he'd tell you how to make them go away. Every night press half an onion and some lemon juice on your palms, then put your hands in gloves so the acid would start to eat away those knobs. Salt and hot water rags might work, but not as well, and he'd heard from a sailor that in Madagascar the natives called warts "woolies" and smeared them with cornmeal and lard and exposed them to the sun. "Are you sure, Billy Lee," my mamma questioned, "he didn't get that mixed up with cooking techniques?"

"No, ma'am," said Bisher, "no siree. And Old Man Allison—he spits on pennies, then ties them to your hands." I shivered to think of wet copper staining my hands green, melting my flesh.

But warts were just one of the things that Bisher knew, could do. For instance, he knew names, real names of movie stars— Bernie Schwartz for Tony Curtis, Judy Garland/Frances Gumm. "Archie Leach, now that's a laugh," he'd say. "Imagine, Cary Grant!" He knew the made-up names of every level down to grip, and watching a movie with Bisher could be a chore. "Bobby Raymond's his real name," he'd whisper when the villain appeared; "Hers is Susie Moore," when the girlish victim smiled at death. "Oh boy," he'd crow, then clap his hands. "Old Lyman Harkney's playing that soda jerk." And even when the story was spoiled by these outbursts, you didn't mind, but wanted to see old Harkney make a comeback shake. You wanted to know Norma Jean Baker by her real name, even when Bisher would argue against that change. "Now why?" he'd say. "Norma Baker is a good star's name. Norma Talmadge made it. Baker sounds so clean, so why'd she change? Brought her nothing but bad luck, poor kid. Did you know she had a round white bed?" He knew political nicknames too, and was the first person I ever knew to call FDR "Frankie Dee." Bisher said, "His own family did that in the confines of their room. The missus, that's Eleanor, I've heard she called him F. Dee Dee."

And Bisher knew the names of things like knots. He never tied a shoelace, his or his kids', without telling you just what it was: half-splice, granny circle, mariner's wheel, whichever one he'd chosen for that day. Once he macrameed his oldest boy's laces halfway down, naming each loop and twist as he taught the child to tie. It was the same with ties. "Windsor, Crown, Full-Dress, or Brummel Bunch," he'd say, and later, when my dad was old and unable to sort out the ends of his own, Bisher was always there on Sunday mornings "to arrange cravats." "A Fanchon Loop?" he'd ask. My dad would nod, then watch in the mirror as Bisher, shorter, hidden behind him, deftly moved the material into wings.

Names of tools, nails, brads, a half-lug screw, a soft-headed angle iron—all these are in my memory, along with others I never try to find in hardware stores. All are inside dope and fun to know. You can see why children always loved him, wanted to go with him to the Dairy Queen to hear him order "Dope and Dodos two by two" or "Adam and Eve on a raft with a side of down." My daughter loves her hamburgers "dragged through the garden," and she'll eat almost anything if Uncle Bisher says it is "a meal with a story behind it."

I am married to a man who is as different from a Bisher Boaz as any man can be. My Mel is tall, lean, pale, wears wire-rimmed glasses, and is a chemist with hair thinning at the crown. He was appalled at tales of Bisher until he met him, then fell under his spell as hard as anyone. When those two are together I love my Mel more as he tries to slouch his frame down half a foot and bounce tough in Bisher's stride. It can't be done, but I love him for the trying.

Bisher knows what he's about with Mel, teasing, making frogs on my husband's arm, and laughing, scuffling out a foot to kick Mel in the rear. "Break your behind, my old Max. You ain't nothing but a hoked-up cook." He nicknamed Mel "Max" the second day they met. Because, he said, Mel had "the look of Maximilian Schell, or the Emperor of Mexico." My husband, immensely pleased, laughed, betrayed himself with a blush. He's wanted a nickname all his life, not just Mel; a shortened version of your name is not enough. Years ago, at a summer camp, he'd tried to start a nickname of his own. Tall and awkward at first base, he'd chatted up his teammates, addressed himself as "Stumpy," encouraged the others to do the same, but Stumpy didn't stick. Until Bisher's baptism, my Mel remained just what he was, a two-syllable Jewish boy good at math and "chemicals." As "Max" he expands in blue jeans that fit rather than cling oddly to his waist, and the whole of him is revved up by Bisher. He's sparked. He starts making lists and listing things as "Number 1."

Oh, Bisher's lists . . . he has one for everything: ten famous redheads, five deadly Arizona snakes. When my daughter squeals, tumbles backwards on the grass, hurling her legs over her head to show cotton bloomers with a ruffled hem, I know if Bisher were here he'd have her on a list. "Want to hear a list of five famous women who showed their private pants in public places? Number 1: Marilyn Monroe on a hot-air grate in New York City, 1956." And the names remain, for Bisher nicknamed everyone. Ellen had a dozen or more, but "Mistress Mellow" was the one she liked the best. I was "Grits" because "You love 'em, you're full of 'em, and your warts feel like 'em." Far from being insulted, I loved that name, signed "Grits" to papers until I was married. My mother was "Miz Matty Mustard," my dad was "Mr. Chaps." Every friend that Bisher had was changed, renamed. Frail Danny Sells became "Dan, the Panic Man" who tried feats like hanging from a window ledge at noon, while C. C. Collins, a druggist in his daddy's store, was called "Chuckles Capistrano, that fine chap," and he grew to specialize in oily giggling. Bisher had nicknames for every pet he met. "Here, Wolf," he'd coax and our old collie Fred would try to growl, and then he'd croon, "Hey, Big Rufus Red," as he stroked our orange striped tomcat Sam.

But what I always loved the best was to listen to Bisher talk about all the places that he'd like to have been. He knew those nicknames too, and the way that the natives said them, like Newpert News and San Antone. I loved the ones that ended in a liquid *a:* Miama, Cincinnata, Missoura, or when he'd give you a choice of pronunciation, say between Nawlans and New Orleens. My favorites always were the "Sans": Peedro, San Jo, Frisco, San Berdoo.

I have often wondered what it would be like to make love to Bisher, or one of his type, and even, on occasion, have worked myself into a frenzy over this. In those early days I watched Ellen with a discerning eye that only sisters have, to see if what she and Bisher did "showed." On her it did. She was and is a woman who is lush, not fat but full, and her skin glows. A man would have to want those deep wide breasts, those soft round thighs that show you she's a natural blonde. Sometimes I wonder who it was I envied most: Bisher, sinking into her to be subsumed, or Ellen, having him with all life's energy.

But for all my dreaming I am aware that Ellen's not had an easy time of it with Bisher being like he is. It's a funny thing that there are men who zero in on a woman they want, as the only thing in life they'll ever want, and once they've gotten her, they start to roam. My husband sees Bisher's episodes as excess energy or misdirected compassion—Bisher's attempts to help some poor girl out. Beginning with advice, he always ends up in bed.

Ellen realizes that these lapses don't mean anything, that she is secure in her position of Number 1. The problem is that it still hurts. She cries her eyes out over each new blonde, and each year I settle down to write a letter telling her that once again all will be well, that Bisher will behave, realize the error of his ways, not to pack her bags and move out here to us, not to storm the honky-tonk, not, whatever else she does, to go to the hussy's house to fight it out with her. Above all, I write, just be calm, you've been through this before. Take up guitar, I urge. You've always had a pretty voice, you like to sing, Bisher likes to hear you sing (not that that matters, I say with an exclamation mark), and that will turn your thoughts away from what is going on at Ruby's Watering Hole. Just get through it, Ellen, one more time. You know you are his everything. And all my love. Then, because I know Bisher would be hurt—and, oddly enough, so would Ellen if I left it out—I add, P.S. Give our love to Bisher but hold off giving it to him for a while.

It always seemed to me that the love story of my sister and Bisher should have high drama in it: a shooting outside The Broken Spoke with Boaz slumping down, wounded in a limb, to be lifted into the back of a pickup truck and jolted into town to have the lead removed. I've pictured that scene a thousand times: Ellen in a cotton dress, shivering in the air-conditioned corridor, waiting for a word about her man, and, at the other end of that linoleumed aisle, a swinging door behind which sits the hussy who has caused it all. She's a brassy blonde wearing stretch pants and patent go-go boots, but close up, to complicate things, her eyes are tired and vulnerable. It would be her ex-husband, released from Huntsville on a 2–10, who shot Bisher down, and that man's now cuffed and crying in the city jail.

But even as good a character as Boaz was, he couldn't make his fate a better story, and I always find the ending sad, the way it petered out. Finally, it was just what you'd expect of anyone—not a Bisher Boaz genius with all his sweet teenaged love. It was one blonde too many, and too trashy, and then it wasn't bearable any more. Ellen couldn't laugh, as she'd once done, at the tales of woe they'd tell Bisher and he'd repeat to her as to why he'd got involved. Although he'd hardly aged, had stayed almost as trim as his boyhood self, he was older now and should know better. He should think of the kids, be more considerate of her. By now Ellen was wider, heavier, her tolerance covered over by both knowledge and flesh. So they were divorced, like one out of every four, and within the year my sister married a widower, a vet who wore pastel polyester leisure suits and had chains dangling on his exposed chest (he is another type who deserves a story of his own). But he seems to love Ellen about as much as he does Samoyeds, and she seems quite content. As for Bisher, within a month he'd married his latest blonde craze, who promptly hung up her dancing pumps, let her hair go brown, and started in making meringue pies with too much tartar in the gelatin.

On our first visit home since the divorce, Mel said he wanted to go see Bisher and I could come if I thought Ellen wouldn't mind, but he meant to go anyway. At breakfast Ellen said she didn't mind, that she saw Bisher almost every day or so to discuss the kids, or just to talk. Pouring coffee for us, she flushed, glanced at the empty place where the vet would sit except he had to attend the birth of puppies, and said, "You know that Bisher. He's always got the inside dope on everyone."

We drove out to see Bisher at his station, and I stayed in the car because it was so hot out there on the concrete where Mel and my ex-brother-in-law were sparring, making plans to go fishing on the coming Saturday. Then, suddenly, Bisher was walking over to the car. Smiling, he leaned into the window frame and said, "Give me a kiss, sweet Grits," and offered me his sweet wet lips. I inhaled that old smell of him: sweat and nicotine and gasoline and the lotion of Old Spice and Lava soap, and began to cry. "Oh Bish," I blubbered, and he said, "Now, Grits, don't cry." As he massaged my shoulder blade, I heard him say, "Got a brand-new list of five dark men who married blondes and then went wrong. Number 1: Joe DiMaggio." Then we three laughed. That night in bed beside Mel, knowing Ellen and her new man, whose hands smell of Lysol and dog hair, are down the hall, I wondered again of sex and love and Bisher. How can she bear it? I thought. To know somewhere not far away he is in bed, in love with someone else who listens to his whispering of names like Frisco, Nawlins, San Berdoo?

Leaving town, we swung by the station to beep good-bye to Bisher. As we honked, drove off, and left him standing on the platform next to the pumps, I saw he didn't wave.

"The Arapahoe Indians invented waving bye—did it backwards to their own faces" was the first piece of inside dope he'd ever told me. And so Bisher never waved good-bye. Instead he bobbed his head. Now, this morning, he nodded us away, as if to say it was his energy that moved the engines of our lives.

Marva Jean Howard
Confesses

At 5:45 in the morning the men at Reilly's Cafe heard her coming. Her clogs sounded like coconut halves in a toddlers' band as they clomped past in cadence. John Gee, sitting by the window, said, "It's that girl from Brady's Boarding House. She's walking toward the jail."

She marched steadily down the middle of the street, tick-tocking her way up to the jailhouse steps, paused to impatiently push at her hair, then walked up and pushed open the door.

Inside, Deputy Sanchez, feet on the desk, was cleaning his fingernails with his penknife, matchstick poking out of his lower left jaw.

"Yeah?" he said.

"I don't want to talk to you. I want to talk to the Sheriff," she said, pushing her hair behind her ears, giving it an angry tug as if to say, "Stay there."

"He's not in."

"Call him."

Sanchez put his feet down. The chair plopped flat. "What for?" He rose, advancing toward the divider that marked the waiting bench from where he was.

"I want to confess to a murder," she said, then pulled an errant strand of hair forward and sucked on it.

"You what!" Sanchez jabbed himself in the hand with his knife trying to put it down and find his ballpoint. The matchstick in his mouth bobbed till it fell.

"Listen here . . ." the girl said, then sighed exaggeratedly, pulled her sweater down, turned, and walked a little ways off.

The Purchase of Order

She's got the longest legs I ever saw, Sanchez thought, and the tightest pants. She looked like a blue wishbone walking. Then she turned, brought her chin sharply to her chest, and said, over crossed arms, "I want to confess a murder, and if, in fifteen minutes, the Sheriff ain't here, I'm saying bye-bye and catching the bus to L.A."

"What's your name?" stuttered Sanchez.

"I'm not talking to you." She sat on the bench, legs stretched out across the aisle. She seemed to be perching on the small of her back, her arms still crossed, her hair around her collarbones. It fell in corrugated waves and was the color of pumpkin pie. She glared from under too-long bangs.

Sanchez rocked back and forth, found his pen underneath his *Racing Bible* magazine, and tried to think what to do with her. He could put her in jail. There was nobody in there but Jeters, sleeping off a drunk. He could call Deputy Assistant Larry Cline, who was supposed to be out on the highway but who Sanchez knew for a fact—he glanced at the clock which said ten of six—was at this moment at Reilly's getting donuts. Did he dare call the Sheriff? That man never did come in until noon. Sanchez didn't know how he'd got elected, somebody's pull, he guessed.

"Hey, dreamer," she yelled. "Fifteen minutes!" Then she stomped her clogs. When she drew up her knees to clasp them, she looked like an ironing board.

Sanchez got on the walkie-talkie. "Roger over," he called. He loved this part of the job best. "Come in, Hot Shot. Bug Bear calling." He and Larry liked to switch around radio names to fool folks with CB's. He thought Hot Shot would call Larry in.

"I said the Sheriff, not no Dukes of Hazzard look-alike." She was at the counter again, at least six feet of her up and down, ten inches wide. CLOMP. She kicked the counter with her clogs and made the ashtray shake. Blowing upward, she got rid of the hair wisps in her eyes.

Marva Jean Howard Confesses

Sanchez, who'd only just made the 5′7″ height regulation, gripped the mike like a gun, laid his hand on the hip where a holster would be if he didn't always take it off because it dug into his ribs and he couldn't ever get comfortable, popped his Dentyne.

"I'm calling the deputy assistant," he said, low and tough.

She spun a full whirling circle, cracked her hands flat on the counter, spatting papers to the floor, silently mouthed "Fifteen minutes," then said aloud, "or L.A." She slap-slipped her hands together, popping the top one off. It hovered in the air, headed west.

Just then the door burst open. Larry Cline, cowboy hat pushed back, both hands holding cups of coffee, a bag of donuts clenched between his teeth, pushed in.

BANG, BANG! barked her clogs. She aimed her index finger at Larry's middle, said, "You're dead."

He almost fainted but kept the donuts high, although he spilled the coffee.

"Slip me a donut ring over this finger," she commanded.

Larry, khaki pants wet with coffee from the knees to the floor, was half in love already. He approached her trotting, bag of donuts bobbing, like a float a fish is teasing with.

"Take the damn donuts out of your mouth," shouted Sanchez. "This woman is a killer."

Larry let his jaw loose and the bag dropped gently into her outstretched hand. She opened it, looked in and took a twist and a chocolate-covered cake, and handed the bag sideways to Sanchez, not looking to see if he was near enough to take it.

"A killer? Who'd she kill? The way they work you at that Brady's you don't get time to kill," Larry said, shaking his boots just the tiniest bit to get coffee out of his toes.

"What do you know?" she said. "You're not the Sheriff." She turned her back to him and began eating her donuts, a nibble off the twist, a crunch of the cake, chewing methodically, keeping them even.

"Did you call the Sheriff?" Larry asked Sanchez.

"No, I didn't. I knew you'd be coming in and thought maybe we could handle this ourselves." Sanchez is filled with the idea of importance now that he thinks he could beat her at arm wrestling if she tried for a getaway. She was making no move.

"Well, I'd call him," said Larry. "You know how he is."

"I'll try." Sanchez went to the desk and first set out the donuts on an open magazine. "There's lots more here," he offered. The truth was he was afraid to call the Sheriff at home; no one ever knew how that man would react.

The girl moved back to lean against the rail and let a big long sigh poke her lower lip out. Larry, who she'd stepped around without a glance, slumped down on the bench. All was quiet except the sound of Sanchez shaking the powdered sugar out of the sack and Jeters in the back just beginning to rouse. He kicked the wall and creaked his bunk every now and then.

They were aware of the door being opened when a breeze blew in. The Sheriff, in fresh-starched and ironed work tans, entered. With one quick flickering of his eyes he took in the girl, now sitting on the rail that separated the jailhouse from his office, Sanchez balancing donuts on a tray of *Racing Bible* magazine, and Larry sitting hangdog on the bench. He also noticed that Larry was either sick or in love, and that his pants were wet from the knee down.

"What's happened here?" he asked calmly, paddling with the toe of his boot the khaki-colored pool that sat right in the middle of the entryway.

"Cline spilt the coffee," blurted Sanchez, offering the Sheriff the side of the magazine that held the jelly-filled donuts.

The Sheriff took a lemon. "I can see that." He bit in and neatly licked off yellow jelly from his lip. "Who's that?" He nodded to-

Marva Jean Howard Confesses

ward the girl, who now straddled the rail, legs so long her knees were bent, clog feet flat on the floor, the length of her subtly vibrating. She nodded back cooly, pulling the corners of her mouth down in a "so-what" moue.

"It's that girl from Brady's Boarding House," said Sanchez, trying to get the Sheriff to take another donut.

"Get those damn things away from me. One of those a month could kill a man."

Sanchez jumped back, powdered sugar sifting to the floor.

The Sheriff forded the coffee, passed Larry, clapping him on the shoulder, saying, "Sit up, man," and approached her.

She slowly swung her leg up and over to sit, both legs dangling down, hands holding the rail on either side. Her stare was reeling the Sheriff in. They would be level if she stayed like this. She did.

"Out with it, Miss."

"Are you the Sheriff?"

"I'm not no goddamn deliveryman," he yelled. "What's going on in here? What's been happening?"

"I came . . ." She leaned back, thighs flattening out. She talked over her rib cage, her hands gripped the rail. It creaked, then groaned.

"Sit up, young lady, you're destroying state property," the Sheriff told her.

"Icametoconfessamurder," she said fast as she snapped up to sit erect.

The Sheriff's eyes went gray and glinty.

". . . And no one here will listen to me. Besides, I said I'd wait for you." She rocked back, then up, then smiled a thin snake smile.

"Who'd you do away with, then?" The Sheriff reached out in the air for the last jelly-filled. Sanchez served it up with a rustle.

"I'm not sure you'd understand," she said. She rocked back

again, then up, then over. She was a saddle hanging on a nail.

"Try me."

"Well . . ."

Larry blurted, "She didn't kill nobody. You only got to look at her. I been looking every day at lunch to know she wouldn't kill nobody."

He'd fallen in love with the way she emptied ketchup bottles, one into the other, constructing little towers that dripped slowly as she wiped tables, filled sugar shakers, and put rice kernels into the salt. While she rarely smiled any more than that thin stretching, still she'd always been polite to Larry and given him his seconds on iced tea fast. She was the only woman he'd ever met who looked like him, but he didn't realize that. He knew only that Marva Jean (a name he'd read on her name tag and said silently as he ate his Blue Plate Special)—her length and lean- ness, her unruly copper hair, and now this, her staunch defiance in the face of law—made him feel complete, fulfilled.

"She couldn't kill anymore'n I could," he said.

She shot him a glance, then said to the Sheriff, "What's your sign?"

"I'm an archer," interrupted Sanchez. "That's a happy man, cause if he can't shoot you with his arrow he can kick your ass with his hooves."

"Shut up," the Sheriff commanded.

"See, I can only confess if our signs are right." She was all the way over now, point of her butt barely touching the rail, the rest of her bent double, her long hands clutching her toes.

The Sheriff squatted, spoke to her ankles. "I'm a Taurus, and that's bull."

"Are you making fun of me?" she asked through a curtain of hair.

"Who'd you kill, girl? And why? Out with it. Let's cut this shit- ting around."

Marva Jean Howard Confesses

She curled down, a thin innertube meeting the floor with a whisper. Then said, "O.K. But just promise, just say you won't laugh, because too many things have happened to me. I couldn't take laughs."

Larry's foot slipped out and paddled in the coffee.

"Clean that up, damn it," shouted the Sheriff. "No, we won't laugh. No lawman laughs at murder."

Sanchez had the official book out and licked his ballpoint pen until his tongue was blue.

"Go ahead."

"I'm Marva Jean Howard," she began, then rose, towering over them all except Larry, who sat, both shoes communing with the coffee pool. She turned to lean slantwise against the wall as though waiting to be frisked. "Though you know me as a person who waits tables at Brady's Boarding House, that ain't me at all."

"Who'd you kill? And why?" the Sheriff prodded.

"Don't you have any sense of ceremony? Or of proper action at all?" she demanded. "How can it matter to you what I've done if you don't know who I am?"

"Every time there's a break-in, I don't ask the booger who done it his life story," said the Sheriff, a touch of defiance in his tone.

"And maybe you should, you might learn something," she shot back.

"You're wonderful," murmured Larry.

"All right, all right," she said angrily, "I'm ready. I'll only say it once cause it's too painful to repeat."

Sanchez wet his pen.

She began: "My name is Marva Jean Howard and I am in the employ of Burleigh and Claire Brady at their boarding house where I wait tables and do housework in exchange for salary and my room and board. I was eighteen years old in March and I never finished high school. My nearest relative is my mother Danita Rice who lives at Las Consuelas Apartments #6, at 1752

San Quito Avenida in Terlengua, Oklahoma." She took a long breath.

"How do you spell Burleigh?" asked Sanchez.

"Is that all the damn far you got?" yelled the Sheriff.

"No, no, I got it all—just not correct. Maybe we should get out the tape recorder."

"I smell donuts," yelled Jeters.

Larry rose from the bench, passed by Marva, who didn't look at him, and took a napkin-wrapped glazed toward the back. Marva then lined up her chin with her shoulder, like an Egyptian frieze, and watched Larry with her long eye.

"Here it is," Sanchez said triumphantly. "Now where's a cassette?"

The Sheriff studied Marva up and down, looking for traces of blood or evidence of gunpowder on her fingers or any signs of violence. Sanchez was testing 1–2–3 when the Sheriff winked at Marva. She stretched her mouth over her teeth and looked away.

"All set." Sanchez clicked it on.

"Although some might not believe me, might think I'm confessing for reasons of attention or publicity, they'd be wrong." She twitched her nose toward the Sheriff. "My story is a sordid and a sad one, so I'll be brief. My mother couldn't keep me, though she tried. I stayed with her until I was seven years old. We had a hard life. Danita needs a man. She can't help it. My daddy, who I never knew, died in a motorcycle crash in Arizona. Danita says if it weren't for that they'd have got back together. So then I lived with cousins, but they had trouble with their own JD's."

Sanchez took notes to supplement the record; Marva sat straight as if on the witness stand. All this rolled out of her as though memorized.

"So then I went to foster homes. In one the woman pretended to be nice, then slapped me around if I asked for the least little thing. Danita got me out of there. Then I spent some time with one of those families—the More-the-Merriers—they always write up in the Sunday papers, but they never did keep you unless you was in a wheelchair."

Larry, who'd come up front again, leaned over the divider, goofy with love as Marva continued.

"I ran away twice in my life. Once to Six Flags in Dallas cause I wanted to and another time to my daddy's mother in St. Joe, Missouri. She called Danita to come get me cause she had cataracts and rheumatism and wasn't prepared to take on a teenager." Marva rolled her eyes back white and made her fingers crooky to show what bad shape her granny was in. "Then the Bastrop Home for Girls, then Brady's Boarding House, where they signed for me until I was eighteen, but then I didn't have nowhere else to go, so now here I am confessing to a murder. That's me in a cracked nutshell."

"That's your confession?" asked Sanchez.

"No, that's who I am." She cut a quick look at the Sheriff. "Now when I confess you'll get a sense of how it was."

"I will," the Sheriff said.

"I will," echoed Sanchez.

"I will," whispered Larry. He was practicing vows.

"See," Marva said, "I finally had to get away. I knew where Burleigh kept the keys so I set the alarm to go off sooner. We're usually up by four, popping biscuits in during the next half hour. So I'd get up a little earlier and no one the wiser."

They could see it: Marva rising in the dark, slipping on her clothes, picking up the clogs which she clung to, and tiptoeing down the stairs. She shushed the dog and stopped the keys from jangling by a tight hold, then cut out to the cool dark that was already beginning to melt into light around the edges. She hobbled over the gravel, walked down to the road where Burleigh's old Pontiac was parked. It chug-chugged quietly, then caught, and Marva Jean Howard was off in the hour before dawn without lights until she was far down the road.

"It was wonderful." She twists over now and tries to make

them understand. "To just be by myself, nobody along, in the dark, and the radio on, and the dashboard lights cheery and no one calling me to come do this or go do that. I thought, you know, Marva Jean, you could go to California this very minute if you wanted to."

Larry's head jerked up in disapproval but then was caught by the wistfulness in Marva's voice, which softened as she talked of her getaway.

"Who has not known the love of oiled leather seats and a lit dashboard," the Sheriff muttered under his breath.

"And a full gas tank," added Sanchez.

"It was beautiful," Marva said.

"We're all agreeing, darling," Larry said.

"Don't darling me, John Law!" She snapped her head fast. That rusty hair flapped out, flared like a firecracker.

"So there I was on Farm Road 2270, riding along. I didn't see another car, and thinking only fifteen minutes more, thinking maybe I'll just ask Burleigh if I can drive the car every now and then to go to Andice and get my hair done, or to the movies or something like that, and the road in front of me, but I'm not thinking about that and . . ."

"Oh no," prayed Sanchez. He could see what was coming. He wondered why no one had called.

Oh no, Larry thought, then said, "Farm 2270 is a bitch. We all know that."

The Sheriff said, "Go on."

"So I was dreaming, no excuse, right? Dreaming that I was somewhere else, and someone else, and then I hit the rise . . ." Marva stood at attention, her hands on that phantom wheel. She hits the rise and her head tilts back.

"And on the other side, they was everywhere—cattle, cattle, cattle—everywhere I looked. I tried to slow down, but I was too fast, they was everywhere, like a red dirt flood."

Each man could see them. Who in cattle country has not? Sud-

Marva Jean Howard Confesses

denly a fence is down and the road is covered with stupid mountains trotting along, overgrown and untanned handbags on hooves, bawling and nudging a grill. Everyone knows too what happens if you can't slow down; they make you, taking the grill on their rear ends, slicing their throats on the outside mirror. And all the time, trotting beside the car, mooing and making eyes.

"I was going too fast and I banged right into one. He was trotting right at me, like he knew me. I honked the horn, he mooed, then I hit him, and he went down." Marva covered her mouth. Her eyes were haunted. "He looked like a big old teepee laying right in the middle of the road."

She hiccupped and Sanchez quickly brought her a paper cup of water.

"Thank you." She sipped gingerly, then regained herself. "So that's that. I knew, sitting there, and then after, when I got out, that my life had ended. There was nothing to do but give up and confess. I'd messed up Burleigh's car, and the cow I killed weren't ordinary."

"How so?" asked the Sheriff, frowning.

"It was Chuckie," she whispered. "The Prince Supreme of Sunrise—that prize bull."

"CHUCKIE!" all three men shouted. "Here, here," Jeters joined from the jail. The Sheriff paced in agitation, Sanchez got another cone of water, and Larry went and touched her elbow. She jumped away and then, in one swift stride, stood on the bench pointing up.

"Yes, Chuckie, the Prince Supreme. I killed him and my name is mud and my future here is done for. Might as well hang myself now," she said fiercely, lifting her right arm up. She looked like Olive Oyl doing the Statue of Liberty, only sad.

"Chuckie." The Sheriff mulled over the name. "Where is he now?"

"Once I saw I couldn't help him I patted his broke neck, then drove away. Threaded through the rest of those steaks on legs, parked Burleigh's car with a windshield note that said "I'll explain," and came right here. I knew if I worked at Brady's plus another job for the rest of my life and saved all my tips till I got Social Security, I still couldn't never pay for Chuckie."

"Not to mention his stud," added Sanchez.

She darted a glance down. "That too, of course. Once Chester Wright finds out that Chuckie's dead and that I killed him, I'm a goner." She squatted down, hunkered on the bench. Larry sat beside her. She used his shoulder like an armrest.

"Prince Chuckie looked like Chester Wright," Sanchez said.

"I never did like Chester," added the Sheriff.

"Too bad it weren't him." Larry cracked his gum and knuckles.

Marva sat between her legs, body slung like a pot in a holder, her face in her hands. If she could have cried, she would, but Marva hadn't cried since she was eleven. She wouldn't start now.

"So what'll I do?" she asked, looking at each in turn, then plopped the length of her out of the hunker and splayed out on the bench like a piece of rope unraveling. She looked defeated and tired. The Sheriff skirted the coffee to come sit beside her.

Marva raked her fingers into her hair and pulled it back tight. Her face was pale, the freckles russet dots that stood out clearly. With her sandy lashes and brows and eyes a watered blue with pink rims, she looked like she'd got out of a swimming pool. She blinked, then blinked again.

"I feel like I want to say 'Where am I?' in some movie mystery." She dropped her hair and crossed her hands on her lap. The Sheriff patted her knee; Larry clenched his fists.

"Like, where am I? And where have I ever been?" She looked bewilderedly around the room, at everywhere but Larry.

"Lots of folks kill cows," the Sheriff consoled. "It's almost a national pastime around here."

"I'd kill 'em myself if I could," blurted Sanchez, thinking that cows always did make him mad, flattening down fences and dirtying up his new mudguards with that stringy cow flop.

"That's not the point," Marva explained patiently. "I used to be a vegetarian, and mostly still am, except for a chicken fried steak now and then. It was just . . . I can't get those eyes out of my head. Brown just like Danita's." Marva's face began to pull in near her chin. Her eyes glistened. "Then I recognized that it was Chuckie from where he'd been on display at the fair when I represented Brady's as a milkmaid."

They remembered her being as out of place as a hat rack in the company of mufflers. But she was the only girl there brave enough to pat Chuckie on his hump, though she wouldn't smile for the photographer sent from Fort Worth. Jeters ran his comb across the bar and played "Show Me the Way to Go Home," while Sanchez blotted up the coffee with old handbills. The Ten Most Wanted faces tanned, blurred in the wet; liquid grew them beards, changing their noses in its wet warp. Sanchez piled up layers of these submerged men, until the Sheriff said, "We might be asked to catch up with one of those guys one day."

"I'm only putting down the ones we got the updates on."

They sat as at a wake, each one hoping for something that could be done, a solution to this fact of Marva's life. Chester Wright was not tractable. Square and stocky as Chuckie, he'd extract his pound of flesh even if Marva Jean had not an ounce to spare.

"I never did like Chuckie," Sanchez said. "Now I know the reason why. He was a troublemaker." Chuckie had been ultimate trouble for Sanchez's brother's cow Bully Boy, who'd lost to Chuckie at the fair two years running. Finally, they said the hell with feeding this no-good and sold Bully Boy off. Sanchez hoped that he'd ended up as tough steaks in someone's freezer.

"All they ever judge at fairs is the meat," the Sheriff began contemplatively. "They don't test brains. I mean, it's not like Chuckie

The Purchase of Order

was one that could have made Chester that much money. It wasn't like Chuckie could stomp out numbers if you asked him how old you was."

Marva stood up in wonder of this. "Whose cow did that?"

"It wasn't a cow, it was a horse, and it could do all kinds of sums and figures," the Sheriff explained.

"How did it hold the chalk?" Larry asked, glancing at her to see if she thought him clever. He was standing too, fitting himself into her shadow that stretched across the floor.

Marva looked at him pityingly. "Little Man . . ." She stretched up and patted his head. "You need some help."

Larry blushed to a solid column of dusty rose.

"Why should you be blamed if that damn Chuckie wanted to get wild?" offered the Sheriff tentatively.

"Yeah, probably he just wanted to get on with it," added Sanchez. "It couldn't have been fun having to eat all the time so you'd get good and fatter and be forced to breed, and when you give out, get your head bashed in."

Marva tilted her head sideways, thoughtfully.

"Now, how about this?" suggested Larry, looking at her, then away, then down at his hands busy wringing out his pants hem. "We could go ahead and log in that Marva Jean came here to confess, but . . ." He paused. "As a witness . . ." A silence fell.

"To the suicide of a damn cow!" shouted the Sheriff, jumping up off the bench.

Sanchez laughed a big "Whoopee" and began to scribble. "Of course, of course. Chuckie had a death wish—you could see it in his big brown eyes!"

"What's going on in there?" yelled Jeters.

"Gonna let you out in a minute," Sanchez shouted back. "Right now we're writing up a report on someone who did hisself in."

"Will Chester take it?" asked Marva Jean.

Marva Jean Howard Confesses

"He's got to," said Larry. "It's the law, aren't we all agreed?" He looked around at the Sheriff eating the last donut, Sanchez writing wilder and wilder, and Marva holding herself like she'd explode.

The two other men nodded, and Marva gave a relieved gasp and folded her arms high like an Indian chief. "Well, thank you. Thank you all very much. Now all I got to worry about is Burleigh's car." She flicked her bangs down over her eyes.

Larry came up and embraced her like he'd carry out the Christmas tree, hands held wide but body leaned away from prickly pine. Then he leaned his head in until their foreheads touched. Their lashes mingled. "Let me take you home," he begged.

Marva's crossed arms were like a TV tray between them. She cocked her head so their noses were next to each other. Now they were so close they were cross-eyed, that sweetest way of seeing.

"I don't have no home," Marva said.

Larry softly puffed her bangs away.

"Let me take you for some scrambled eggs, then," he whispered.

She pursed her lips forward for a moment, then pushed them out farther in a brief kiss that answered "Yes." The Sheriff and Sanchez released the sighs they'd been holding and the room seemed filled with lights and wafts of summer breeze. Larry and Marva stood entwined, two gawky giants, bushes of red hair glowing flamingo in the sun. Then, relaxing her arms, she reached around Larry, took a firm grip on his back, and slowly they tangoed out the door.

Doing Yoga

Dotty Schneider lost her job at the Community Health Center when they ran short of funds and, I suspect, saw she was expanding her territory into holistic health. Small and wiry, she had one of those faces that far away make you think you'll meet a teenager, but up close you see wrinkles surrounding the apprehensive look of a monkey. Her hair was either pulled slick-back or unleashed to flow, black, with gray streaks, over her shoulders. She dressed dramatically, all white on top, a collection of Victorian slips, prairie skirts, and drooping Juliet-sleeved blouses over starkest black tank-top leotards, muscle-cut so that when she bent in bows her breasts rose over the edge. Not seductively, because hers were yogi's breasts, which is to say like two fried eggs without the shimmer of a yolk.

Dotty was given to grabbing your upper arm and whispering intently about eating habits. Her mantras were made up, I know. I always tried to find out what other people's were because mine didn't do a thing for me. Saying "Cork, cork, cork" never moved me into space because just the sound of *cork* made me concentrate on popping my tongue against the roof of my mouth, and the harder I tried not to, the more I had to move my lips to make any sounds at all.

Dotty's life was a total mess, and I sometimes thought that was why her yoga classes were so successful. You kept coming to see what horrible thing would happen next. Before and after every class she'd rapidly utter the unutterable: her husband was impotent, she didn't know why. He was her second, a Mexican potter who wore Birkenstocks and who once lived in Arizona caves. "A well-rounded guy," she'd said, "so why can't he?"

31
Doing Yoga

"Now breathe," she said. As we filled our lungs with air, one image of her spouse, now our model for relaxation, held us.

Dotty's toilets were always overflowing, her carburetors cracking, children getting pinkeye and measles, and neighbors acting weirdly. She'd spew this as she pulled off a collection of capes, scarves, wraps, shawls, blankets with openings cut at odd angles. She's the only person I ever knew who's lived in the Northeast all her life and never owned a coat. She'd step out of heel-less Earth shoes, strip off thick wool socks, and stand, feet bare and bony, tensile toes gripping the floor, saying "Enough of me and mine." Then she'd shake her head rapidly from side to side, to drive away the image of that next-door neighbor bent on bothering everyone, but chiefly Dotty, with her bizarre behavior.

Without pause for breath she greeted the sun, stretching up with palms tented, face beatific, eyelids down but not quite closed, her eyes racing rapidly in the space that showed. The pace of her heart was quite visible and at odds with the hypnotic singsong of her instructions: "Breathe, stretch, loosen, and let go," each word distinct, a small hook. It was this metronomic quality that energized me. As others fell into stupors, Dotty's expression on their faces (she insisted you pat the lines around your mouth and puff, whispered, panicky, "No frown, no frown, no frown"), funny images, stories, wild notions lifted me. I was awkward at the moves; my genius lay in being still, standing head slung forward like a peasant awaiting the block. Hoarding secret selves, I kept my eyes slit for what would happen next.

During the middle of every class the gymnasium door creaked open and one of Dotty's kids, or one of their friends, appeared. Never coming all the way in, they stood in the door's slant, like being denied entrance into heaven, and stared silent messages. She'd give us an exercise to occupy both conscious and unconscious minds, and then sidle toward the son, daughter, friend, who was too fat, too thin, lank-haired, pregnant, broken-out, puffy-eyed from tears, and woebegone. All wore the same khaki duffel coat. She pushed at them, but they never went all the way out. The class collectively held its breath to hear fast and furious exchanges: "What did he do to you now?" "You lost your job?" "Where is the baby?"

Each encounter ended in a fresh burst of tears on the part of the pathetic messenger, then shoes shuffled, a hug, I suppose a whispered mantra, the thud of a door. "Release, let go, refresh." Dotty stood before us again, thin, with every part of her upper chest defined, separated like ripples on the sand. Her eyes widened slightly, then bulged as she gave orders to change directions. A fast shake of her head, sometimes a rueful smile as if to share with us these demands, and then another move. We'd sway to the right, legs bent at the knee and pointing left, to twist our navels to our spines. "Pull it out—let it go—it knows where it belongs." Dotty had a theory about twisted umbilical cords getting people off to a wrong start, and so tried to get us all unraveled to face life straight on.

I kept coming. I couldn't stay away. What followed each physical session grew more and more exotic. This group—there were six of us—shared our writing and were encouraged to blurt out lines at random. I made up throwaways so as not to squander written ones. "You say he loves you, but he only buys plantains," intoned one classmate whose husband was in jail for running Bolivian coke. "Wading in ice water to my thighs—aaarrrghhh," screamed a wilderness editor. I, maintaining a pose as sensitive, murmured, "Shades purple shades of night, falling falling."

"Yes, yes," clicked Dotty, propelling us into a circle where we related birth experiences.

Each time I swore never to go again, then did, feeling my compromise, dressing for it, planning for it, wondering if I would choose to be born again. I hadn't done well at primal scream; the corners of my lips cracked and cold sores formed, a punishment of intellect, I knew. Then Dotty announced in her choppy little

Doing Yoga

voice: "Next week . . . special . . . bring best inner selves . . . bless." We all bowed to the sun, moon, various stars, the lines on the gym floor.

I was excited all week and arrived early. Dotty, later than usual, hurried in, dropping layers like leaves or pasts behind her. Into this rubbishy wake strode a statuesque woman with masses of springy dull hair growing in tight waves straight from the scalp. A huge head of hair, almost circular, surrounding a wide flat face with long hooded eyes, a man's broad nose, fleshy Mick Jagger lips: the face of an Aztec priest, utterly blank, utterly merciless.

"Here she is . . . ," breathed Dotty, "Emma Crane . . . the healer." Dotty stood, hands at her side upturned, outstretched, supplicating as she presented us. She usually wanted us to be a good class with flexible bodies and interesting inner lives, but this time what she wanted most of all was for one of us to be sick.

We tried to oblige. You could tell Dotty was impatient with our stuffed-up noses, complaints of tension tightness in the shoulders, and unexplained creaks and cracks in our joints, all supposed to be cured by yoga. Emma Crane was not too happy either. She desultorily passed wide strong hands over the swollen knee, the clubbed and bruised toe, and closed her eyes briefly, either praying or silently saying, "Get me out of here and into a nursing home where I can really go to town." Even while I knew Crane for a fraud, I was impressed with her majestic largeness. Her hands would never fit kid gloves; you couldn't imagine her feet in Cuban heels. These were flat feet meant for dirt yards, fields, maybe toes clinging to a mountainside as she fought for dominance with hawks. She exercised with us too, but her heart wasn't in it. She had a mission to fulfill and we weren't up to it.

The next week, gathered in the gym, stretching, we six discussed this healer and her purposes. "I hear she's really good," said the nature editor. "Lived in Wyoming and raised sheep for ten years." "She's a certified midwife, they say, from Yale." This came from the drugger's spouse, who continued, "Life, birth, sickness, death—it all combines." I lowered my head as always when sentiments like these were expressed, knowing the last speaker once asked me if my dishwasher had a special karma. As we sat pulling over to pull toes back to our insteps, you could feel the wish that someone would walk in who needed such ministry. When a girl I recognized from work, knew only as Sandy, came in, we all turned and stared. Tall, thin, with a dancer's light carriage, she was no one's idea of someone sick. She smiled, sat, crossed feet over thighs, then asked, "Where's the healer?"

"Why?" I didn't mean to be rude, but I didn't understand why anyone would want to join our group.

"What do I have to lose?" She shrugged, then leaned over in a ball to examine the floor. The rest of us grew interested in our knees.

That class and the two that followed I barely recall. Once Sandy swayed in front of Emma Crane as those big hands moved from ankles to throat, pushing up, sliding flesh like you'd push a toothpaste tube to get the last of it. That healer's head faced heaven as her mouth emitted a stream of pure sound, ululating, indecipherable. Sandy's head wagged right, then left; then her mouth fell open, stayed that way for a minute, closed.

Another time we were told to put hands on her. I palmed her instep, pretended it was something round and bony like a turtle; turtles live a long time, hundreds of years. Emma Crane pushed the heel of her hand on Sandy's forehead and shouted, "Out." Another time Sandy cried, said she was afraid. The class murmured, "Don't be, don't be," but Emma Crane contradicted us, commanding, "Be, let fear well up, accept, be afraid." Dotty, circling them, clicking the last word, said, "Afraid," said, "Be."

At the fourth class of healing, Sandy was not there. By then we'd learned the name of her disease. It was that one we all fear, encounter in our dreams, look for in the faces of friends when they mention signals, signs. It is the thing ignored until too late: the pucker in the breast, the mole behind the knee, the cough that wakes us in the night and won't go away. Sandy had had for two years what could no longer be contained. She'd left her job, was at home now, too sick to come to class to be healed.

Soon after, my telephone rang one night. A voice I vaguely recognized said, "Hi. Tell me—what's your mantra?"

"I don't hand out my secret mantra to a voice on the phone," I answered. Then I realized it was Sandy and I felt afraid.

"I'll tell you mine. It's *placemat*," she said. There was a humming silence in the line.

"*Placemat?*" I felt a terrible laugh building in me.

"Yes, *placemat*. Now, tell me how could anybody work up to peace and tranquility with *placemat*? That word is simply impossible. So what's yours?"

"*Cork!*" burst through my nose. I began to snort.

"Oh God." She was laughing. "These are worse than I thought. Jan's is *stub*."

"*Stub?* Where did Dotty get these? She's an idiot," I said.

"Yes, she is. She is. And so is that Emma Crane." Between hiccups of laughs Sandy said, "I can't be healed. I'm dying. I'm going to die. I'm not 'passing to a new stage on a road untrod.' Actually, I wouldn't want to go there if that's how they talk." She sounded lively and feisty, and not in the least sick. "But, you know, I wanted to know other people's mantras just in case. What if mine is the only one that doesn't work?"

"None of it ever works," I said, secure in this knowledge. Hadn't I tried them all, from Rolfing to sweat huts on a mountaintop? "But come back anyway. Be with us. We're a weird old gang. Besides, I need somebody for the yoga partner prize. Now that you know there's really no secret to it, Sandy, come back."

The Purchase of Order

Then I suddenly felt sad, as though maybe in admitting to the blank behind our words murmured and written I'd done something to Sandy, taken away a hope.

There was a long pause. "I'll try," she said. "Sometimes I get so tired. I'll try."

On the next class night the lights are dim. Everyone but me faces a partner. As I stand making my mind blank, cooing "Cor cor cor," my eyes count bleacher tiers. Then the gym door opens and Sandy walks in. No one turns to greet her, clasp her, shout out, embrace. Her footsteps are soft on the hardwood floor with the sound of damp palms pressed together. We are all aware of her progress. Then she faces me. Thin now, so very thin, skin translucent over her hollow temples. I can't believe these frail hands could open doors.

"Now breathe," breathes Dotty. Sandy smiles the smallest smile, mouth barely quirking at the corners as we breathe, exhale, and move to our knees, to breathe, then lower to the floor. I want to look at her again, but don't, afraid the hollows of her collarbones will catch my eyes. We sit, spreading into second position, our upper bodies straight, our legs east-west compasses. "Stretch up and out and lift," chants Dotty as the class lifts arms in wide arcs, smoke signals to the sun, leaning right and left, a weaving dance from hip sockets up.

"Connect." We lean forward from our spines, torsos parallel to wood as we reach out to clasp our hands. Sandy's shoulder blades are fragile as wings, and when we meet it's as if I handled glass; her hands on me are weightless. Sliding palms down elbows, wrists; when our fingers touch, it is the light connection used when testing irons. We breathe in unison.

Now the sound of *cork*, so buoyant, so resilient, so linked with the pop of joyous celebrations, makes every spoken *cork* a privilege. Eye to eye along the floor, sharing the wood with dust, the ground-in smells of tennis shoes, I feel the molecules and cells

Doing Yoga

that make things as finely grained as hardwood floors or double-jointed wrists. Through my half-shuttered eyelids I see Sandy's head lower slightly sideways to extend farther out. If we were seen from above, we'd be a diamond shape, legs splayed to the side, hands touching like supplicants or saints as our torsos skim the floor, breaths mingle.

If I am very quiet I can go lower, longer, heart to beat against the wood, and maybe she'll rise up. I can help her go. She is lifting now, I know it. I form the word *release* and hear Sandy sigh, then open my eyes, only to see that I am the one lifted up.

Flying far away, hovering at the top of the gym, as in the dream I have had over and over all my life, floating through space above the nets, feeling my stomach quiver as it does in an elevator's drop. All my heaviness, my sad purposes are left below. It's curious to see us, paired in design, tents collapsed, with the center pole still yearning upward. I know this dream, if it is a dream, will not allow me to soar and dip; just being up here, seeing us lozenge-shaped is dream enough.

Even as I watch, our legs stretch out, our arms lengthen. If Sandy were released we would be flying. Before I settle back, drift in lazy circles down, her face shows serene and closed. When my eyes open I am surprised to see the backboard and net above me. Sandy is alive and we breathe the air together. Her heart pulses in a regular ropy rhythm through my fingers. Her veins roll under my touch—she is slowly moving her lips and the word *placemat* unfurls like a carpet to heaven.

A Small Hotel

When people tell you your life can change through just one move, I know exactly what they mean. My life completely changed, for both the good and bad, when I walked up the hill to work at the Hotel San Soon. First I met Ms. Cleta Coombs, who is an inspiration, though she drives me crazy with her silly rhymes like "It's confusing but amusing" and other jingles when things are turning sour. She looks a little like Natalie Wood, somewhat soft but vivid, and behind those silly sundresses with sunglasses to match, Ms. Cleta's got fire, ambition, and get-up-and-go.

"How'd she get saddled with Buster?" is something not only my daddy asks.

"He's a Coombs," Mamma said, as if that explained things. The Coombses own a chain of variety stores, but Buster's in the off-line.

"Buster just needs the right direction," Ms. Cleta told me once when we caught him snoozing in the Pawley's Island hammock meant for VIP's. Then she nudged him out sharply with her toe.

"Yes, ma'am," I answered. You don't argue with Cleta when she's got on spikes.

This old hotel is also the place where I met Hobart Gardner Granger III, "Hobie" to those in the know, and the man who, though he's only eighteen, is the epitome of masculinity to me. From the moment I set eyes on him I knew I would do whatever he said, though usually it isn't anything but go get him a Chocolate Soldier and a pack of Nabs.

Here are the reasons I love Hobie: he's the only boy I ever knew who doesn't wear Aqua Velva when he's dressed up; he's not afraid to wear pink shirts and get teased about green and Thursday (other boys don't know what pink does to a man's tan and a crewcut tipped with sun-blonde hair: makes 'em look like a darling porcupine). He read *Dharma Bums* and told me about Kerouac and Cody. He listens to race radio and now I know what Crawling King Snake really means.

Hobie doesn't belong here. He goes to school up East where they wear coats and ties and really take Latin, not like here where all Miss Johnson does is talk about her trip to Rome when she was young about a million years ago and makes you do *amor amat*. He lets me practice giving hickeys on his arm, and sometimes French-kissing if he's in the mood. Hobie never closes his eyes, only pretends he's a mannequin you send for in the mail; that way he'll never get involved. Whenever Beverly Martin walks by in her white bathing suit, Hobie says, "Don't worry, you'll fill out."

The reason he doesn't love me: no breasts. No, that's not fair; he's my friend and I'm too young, too silly, and he says my head's too gummed-up with island stuff that I gotta clear out. This job at the hotel is one step on the road.

When the Coombses started hiring summer staff I became one, and this is what I did: I answered phones, the old-fashioned kind with long cords that pull way out and loop around and plug in holes, and you have to keep saying, "Excuse me, I thought you were on another line." I served meals to Orleen, the organist, while she played for the fashion shows, slipping the plate of scalloped potatoes with ham chunks in on the right, not too near to her music. I collected all the towels left in sodden heaps around the swimming pool and took them across to the Suds & Duds. The machines at the San Soon were always breaking down, and if the guests asked you for another towel you were to tell them they were on Spin. I dragged towels across the street, shoved dimes into the dryer, folded them up, and took them back as is.

The Purchase of Order

"Only wash it, if there's a stain," Ms. Cleta said. I threw cracked corn into Ali McCaw's cage, set out plastic cups and Cheezits for the afternoon refreshments on the walk-through, and hunted down Ping-Pong balls that disappeared as fast as that bird's corn.

My worst task was helping Ms. Maudrey Bridges set up the Island Art in the lobby, because she jangled her bracelets real loud and asked me to comment on the works. As far as I could tell, they were all horrible, and all painted by her under a bunch of made-up names. Then Bridges'd bring things down from Macon where her granddaughter Carmalee did little glued-on woods that featured seagulls or shacks on stilts.

Once I had to scrub out a tub for a guest who was mad because the toilet seat didn't have a paper strip across it. She said the whole place was unclean. She sat on the edge of the bed, legs crossed at the knees, swinging her feet in plastic sandals, and her toenails looked hard, yellow, and filthy. I scrubbed the tub blazing white with Bab-O and got not a tip nor even a thank-you. Ms. Cleta blames that cleaning call on a marriage spat; I was the poor bone that got tossed into it and she was the one who did the tossing.

"Well, why did you?" I asked her. She replied that the maids were off and she couldn't do everything. She did a lot too, but usually was to be found in the kitchen helping cut carrot curls while Buster, that slick-headed goon, hugged up to the law enforcers when they came for conventions.

However, Buster did warn me about the Sound Wave Church of Jesus. We almost had two fires while they were here for their reunion. They mainly stayed in their rooms and conversed on walkie-talkies. They were people used to being alone, calling in questions about Scripture late in the night, and doing things in person made them nervous. They laughed too loud or ordered peanut butter and jelly when it wasn't on the menu. Mainly they saved money by stacking up eight to ten to a room and trying to heat up feasts in a hot pot. You could smell noodle soup up and down the corridors. Buster had a general announcement he made at least twice a day: "The Hotel San Soon is not a boarding-house. There is no cooking in the rooms, there are no unauthor-ized guests in the rooms, there is no . . ." Whenever he couldn't think of anything else to add, he'd say, "There is no forward be-havior in the rooms."

All the Sound Wave Church folks would bend their heads and listen more intently to their cassettes, or duck underwater if they were in the pool. Not one of them went into the ocean for a swim, that I could see, although bunches of them walked up and down the edge of the water, trousers rolled up to the knee and dress hems pulled back to front like in India. In the mornings it re-minded you of the Sea of Gallilee, seeing them out there in the mist, wading around and saying their prayers out loud.

Now this Hotel Annual Gala we're doing is Ms. Cleta's in-vention. She plans to make this the start of something like the Mardi Gras. She invited all the groups to join us—the island Brownies and the Weebelows, Prepared and Aware, and July Fourth Exhibitors, plus every other organization that could muster two members. She could be president of the U.S. or at least mayor of Brunswick if she put her mind to it; she's that organized. She's offering everyone lobby space for their arts and crafts handiwork, and outdoor booths for baked goods and paintings of Elvis on velvet and a photo column in the *Sand-tracks*, the island weekly where she writes "The Piper." There's a good response and the Chamber of Commerce and the banks are giving the blue bunting for the outdoor booths, and the library's gonna stay open till five and display books by local poets and lorists and others on shells and luaus.

However, Ms. Cleta's getting miffed because no one wants to perform, not even the Bottle Band, which usually you can hardly stop from phtting and huffting their Pepsi tunes. "We'll have to do all the acts ourselves, I guess," she fumed. She suspects that Miss Mindy's behind this reluctance because they have a long-ago recital grudge having to do with Chinese splits.

"She's just keeping them out," Ms. Cleta muttered. Then, "Do you dance?" she briskly asked me one Saturday as we folded sheets.

"No, I don't," I answered firmly. She's got something on her mind, all right. Poor Gay Lee, I think she knows how to do the shuffle-hop-ball change along with the hula. She'd better start practicing.

No one on the San Soon staff wants to do any acts either, but everyone has to, or get fired, so like any bad deal you rush in and get the best one you can. Hobie's gonna be the emcee because he's the only one without an accent, Marsha and LaMona will be the costume coordinators, Orleen will choose the music, the Chef gets to sing solo, and the staff all together sing "Banana Boat" and the Coke ditty. Ms. Cleta pushed for "A Spoonful of Sugar" and "Climb Ev'ry Mountain" because Julie Andrews is an idol of hers, but all the cleaning staff was practicing "Day-o, Day-o" already.

On the afternoon of the assignment of the acts, we all line up. Gay Lee *can* do the hula, but she does it so timid her grass skirt hangs straight as hair. She keeps laying her head over to one shoulder and smirking her mouth odd in a style she thinks Hawaiian.

Ms. Cleta says, "I think—no, dear."

Gay Lee looks relieved. Now all she'll have to do is carry the banner and play "Bumblebee Boogie" on her flute.

Ms. Cleta's head swivels, taking us in. Hobie says smoothly, "I couldn't do anything else but announce. I need to give the acts continuity." That's how you get to be emcee. Know words like "continuity" and go to school up East so you don't sound corny, and wear a real white dinner jacket and not a white sports coat. He's even got pants with a stripe down the leg and is making up a Perry Como patter.

"I'm learning how to juggle," LaMona says. I think with knives; that's how her hands continue to get cut.

"Ms. Cleta . . ." It's George with his deep round voice. "Us in the kitchen will sing an island song, and excuse me, I've got to go and check the entrees now."

Once I went down to the end of the island where George and all his family live to deliver something Ms. Cleta said he had to have. I came up on my bicycle and they were all sitting on the back porch, watching the egrets flit out over the yard. The sky was purple and the trees hung moss and you smelled woodsmoke where they'd cooked out. Lotte's grandbaby patted the dust with her hands and it was so quiet and peaceful that I wanted to stay, but I wasn't invited. They gave me a drink of grape soda pop, and Creighton said he'd load me on the pickup if riding back in the dark was too much for me. I said it wasn't. On the way back, with my front light making a small cone of yellow, I thought that the moss was reaching down to me; I thought I didn't want to have to be riding my bike around in the dark delivering messages for Ms. Cleta, and how I wanted to be an egret, white and frail with a swoopy neck, darting down to scoop up whatever it was they wanted and then soaring away. I thought how I wanted to stay on that porch and not worry about my daddy's new job or my mamma's tears, and how I couldn't. Hearing George's voice made me think back on all that, and *that* is why I wasn't alert to what was happening as I stood in this circle listening to Ms. Cleta organize to change our lives.

Ms. Cleta is tapping her foot, the big toes pushing impatiently out of the openwork shoes. Her toenails need painting again, and I'll be the one to do them.

"Deenie?"

The Purchase of Order

I look up. My face is a closed door to her.

"You dive?"

Her voice is a pretend question. She knows I do. Knows it is a pleasure for me. I like to practice flips and fancy falls. I like to cut the air and water when no one's watching. When did she spy on me?

"And Greg does?"

Greg hears his name and smiles wide as a goofy hound. He'd wanted to be the lifeguard but couldn't learn the intricacies of the sign-in sheets. He's Hobie's helper. His tasks include walking slowly around the pool pulling on his whistle, tugging his white shorts down at the thighs, and saying, "You!" followed by short shrilling blasts whenever a bad boy does a cannonball. Mostly Greg's for looks. But he can dive, I've got to admit it. He taught me to backflip two years ago, though I'm beyond him now.

"It's settled, then." Ms. Cleta claps her hands and pats her head like she's adjusting a fur hat. "A diving contest. Girls against the boys. Deenie versus Greg in the Show of the Summer!" She's almost hysterical in her happiness. I think Ms. Cleta must be going through the Change.

"A what?" Greg asks.

"A diving contest, stupid, and I'm not doing it," I say.

"But Deenie, why?" Ms. Cleta's voice throbs with shock. She bends down, pulling her sunglasses to the end of her nose, and peers at me like I'm sick.

"That pool's not deep enough."

"Oh, Deenie, it is too. And you are a good diver. So is Greg. And you two *will* dive. Maybe you can practice something together." She cocks her head. The right half of her hair clomps over her eye; she shakes it back like a flirt. "You'll be our Grand Finale."

"Maybe they could dive with torches," Hobie slyly suggests.

"Or fire batons." This from Gay Lee, who'd always made the

band, never been a twirler, though she's taken lessons from Miss Mindy since kindergarten.

"It's settled, then," announces Ms. Cleta. "Now the only thing we've got to do is practice the staff's Sousa march." We groan around.

"What act are you doing, Ms. Cleta?" asks Hobie.

"I'll be the stage manager, dear," she says, pulling a sweet smile. That means she can hide when things go bad.

"The smocks didn't come down from Savannah yet," says Marsha. She and LaMona got leftover beauty smocks from a chain called Hair Tonique that'd gone out of business. These were gonna be the hotel uniforms and also be cut up into various scraps for the banner and the costumes.

"You can wear my recital blue, Deenie," offers Gay Lee. Like all hopeful twirlers, she has a closet full of sequinned bathing suits with stars and feathers and fur everywhere you don't want any if you are serious about your stretch.

Ms. Cleta wiggles her fingers at me. "Come on, Dog," I say to Greg. He loves me to call him Dog, which I do because he's always after me and I'm not even pretty. Would he take any of the other girls who wore small shoestrings around the pool? No, he's like the scarecrow in *The Wizard of Oz*—he wants brains, mine in particular.

"Be decent to the poor guy," Hobie'd say. "He's crazy for you."

"But why? He's blonde. I'm dark. He's big. I'm little. He's dumb and I'm smart. Besides, I love you." Then I'd give Hobie's forearm a passionate kiss.

"Let go, you're hurting. Opposites attract. And you don't really love me, you only think you do. You've got to grow up yet."

I'd always groan when Hobie said that because he was right. Here was Greg, just my age and loving me too. Why was life so out of whack?

"Come, come, my pieces of resistance," Ms. Cleta calls. She is more right than she knows. "Now this is fun," she says. I study my toes. "In Atlanta this is the latest thing. There are contests and the ones competing don't know until the last possible moment what it is that they'll be doing. Then, as the contest starts, they have to do whatever it is that the crowd says!" She gives a little squeal and a hop. "Isn't it fun?"

"Did you see them do this with dives?" I ask.

"Well, no, but the cutest thing at the Marriott—they had two girls in evening dresses, hoops and all, and they had to do the wildest things, like crawl on all fours to the end of the restaurant and beg for nickels."

"Did you really think we could do dives that way?" She's beginning to get doubts because she's chewing on the inside of her cheek.

"Well . . ." Ms. Cleta pulls in her nostrils the tiniest bit; she's made up her mind. "Deenie, a diver is a diver. After all, they all start the same way—running down the board and hopping into the air. There's a lot of time to change your mind." This from a woman who's only been seen once going off the side of the pool, hair in a mop-of-flowers bathing cap, holding her nose as she jumped feet first.

"It's too dangerous," I mutter.

"All it takes is one competitor with spirit," Ms. Cleta says. "We'll let Greg compete against himself if you think you can't."

"I didn't say I couldn't. I could, and I guess I will, if that's what you want, Ms. Cleta. I'm only glad to think I have my coverage when I end up in the hospital with a broken neck." Then I stalk off with as much dignity as I can.

So the weeks passed with everyone deep in preparation for this fete and reservations coming in heaps from groups that saw a chance to go plumb crazy. We got the Tri-State Sheriffs and the Jazz Dance Groups of the South and the Buddies of Borzois and all the regulars who weren't gonna know what hit them. Any-

A Small Hotel

time, day or night, you could hear the help harmonizing on "I've got to teach the world to sing in perfect harmony," and the men going hm/hm/hmmm in graduated scales. Marsha and LaMona, those dining room inseparables, brought in their sewing machines and zinged away making capes and banners and costume pieces. The kitchen staff practiced in secret and even Hobie was mumbling his patter under his breath. The only ones who weren't practicing were me and Greg.

One night after the weekly drain and scrub of the pool (all the little kids were paid a dime to scrape algae off the bottom while Hobie hosed) I waited until the water was new and clean and blue and then climbed to the high dive. With the pool lights off, I had Hobie shout dives to me in the dark. It felt funny going to the end of the board and waiting. I couldn't get the proper bounce or feeling that went with each preparation. As I came up from one flopper, Greg stepped out of the archway of the Hacienda Conference Room and said, "I want to try." He got to the end of the board after his run and did a huge jump into the air as Hobie screamed, "Jackknife Split." Greg did one—perfect too. Then he came up grinning.

"I think that's what Ms. Cleta wants us to do."

I didn't bother to answer, just walked away. Of course it was. It's only that I didn't like the looks of it, or the feel. I liked to think about my dives, not wait until I was suspended before I decided if I was going up or down.

On the eve of this first gala, the Hotel San Soon grounds were teeming with folks. Under my smock I was wearing one of Gay Lee's more modest achievements, a hot pink stretch with a single row of pearls around the top and straps that wouldn't break under the stress of a twist. As the last of the day darkened into night, Ms. Cleta hurried the dining guests out of the Cockle Shell and onto the Wisteria Patio where the waiters scurried around getting drinks. Buster collected the sheriffs to come out and view the show from the Hacienda roof, and the kitchen was in turmoil with a thousand different melodies moving up to mix with steam from the broccoli soufflé.

Ms. Cleta came into the hall where the first batch of us were waiting to lead the parade up to the ridge. "Good luck," she said lots of times. And "Break a leg," which I don't think is nice to say. Then she came over and put her arms around me. She looked real nice in a deep rose gown that was tucked up with flowers on the hem. Her hair was French-rolled and there were little sparkly items in it, and a new false mole pasted on her face.

"Have you forgiven me yet, sweet pea?" she whispered. I smelled White Shoulders and wondered how she ever got with Buster, who was busy fixing his clown suit and smelled of Old Spice.

"Yes."

"I know you'll win," she winked.

Suddenly I wanted to cry. My daddy wasn't even here tonight, out somewhere in the South convincing people to buy Burlington socks with clocks, and though Mamma got a shift off to come, she'd already rumpled her figured chiffon and had two Bloody Marys on my tab. Mamma painted my face with waterproof mascara and lipstick that beads water on your mouth, but it doesn't come off on anything except your teeth. I looked around at all the milling in this hall and wondered what in the world I was doing here.

Orleen struck up the organ and began the Sousa sound, and the front desk and the cleaning staff in nylon smocks of mustard, fuchsia, and lime marched smartly out the doors and around the pool in one big circle, except where the concrete was broken we had to do a little hop. Then we stopped, twirled and walking backward and upward in faltering baby steps, arrayed ourselves in ranks behind the diving board, ranged out on the knoll, ocean to our backs. A steady wind blew in from the sea, shaking the lanterns and casting shadows over the pool. Our smocks billowed like clipper ship sails.

Gay Lee held the banner, a sheet tied, dyed, and embroidered ANNUAL GALA. We started to put FIRST on it when Ms. Cleta said, "No, don't. Cause then we'd have to—one . . ." (counted on her right fingers, bit to the quick) . . . "rip FIRST off next year and maybe make a mess of the banner. Or two . . ." (counted on her left hand, nails somewhat longer and polished with Little Lilac) ". . . have to make another, and that'd be redundant." The banner limped sadly in the evening's breeze, not enough life to it to even fling up once to herald the march of the Security Staff.

Officer Swan led off, belly preceding his gunbelt and guns. Everything that could be polished on him was. He'd even used Pearly Drops on his teeth, although he didn't smile and wouldn't, unless by chance a couple on their honeymoon might decide to make love during the show. Then he'd train his flashlight on them and grin; but no such luck, this was a serious celebration.

Next in line was second in command Dubbie Wells, dressed in a uniform of his own devising: khaki work pants and shirt, black and white hounds-tooth tie, ditto belt, black "gimme" cap from Shedd's Shotgun Shells ("That'll scare 'em," you could just hear the feebleminded Dubbie say) and hightop black and whites. Slung around his waist were these instruments: (1) a canvas canteen about the size of a cantaloupe; (2) a false Swiss Army knife; (3) a three-way flashlight (he had a pinpoint in his breast pocket); (4) a tiny tool set in blue plastic; (5) a whole bunch of keys that didn't open anything, though Dubbie'd try them every time, squatting, sweating in front of the Corvette, the Cougar, the Ford Fairlane, whose owner had locked herself out. Usually she stood nearby, dancing back and forth on the hot asphalt, heat burning through her flip-flops and under her terry towel coverup that Dub would cast poor glances at. He didn't look, but turned his eyeballs up and fluttered those sandy lashes, as he tried to poke a curlicued wrought-iron gate key into a tiny silver space.

"This ain't right either," he'd mumble.

"Oh, Dub," the girl would whine and nudge him with a toe. "I've got a Coke date."

"Huh." He'd pull another useless key out.

Now here he was, walking along with his metal hula fringe, clink-clanking. He and Officer Swan linked up with walkie-talkie ears, muttered into their fists at each other as both paused, pivoted, spun twice, clicked heels, and marched on around the pool like the Jackson Brothers.

Then through the doors came what I called "The First Line of Disgust," what Swan called the "Swan Scouts," in motley of their own and all with flashlights lanyarded to their waists. These were all the weasel-faced boys from eight to eighteen who roamed the beach and bushes for courting couples, gathering evidence: a crumpled Camel pack, a spent shotgun shell, an old Baggie which they'd pinpoint in light and call out to each other about in codes: "COOLA HAY, COOLA HA." Boys the Boy Scouts wouldn't let near a real troop, except maybe overnight when a little evil around a campfire could be considered part of growing up. They were Jackson Brother stepping too, snapping arms and legs and heads as fast as they could and glaring at couples on their wedding nights. Orleen, revved up by the thrill of it, double-timed and moved into the theme of *Walking Tall* or *Billy Jack*.

The knoll was filling up fast and the first smockers started to teeter a little. Of course, some wriggling was necessary as we wondered who'd finally carry in Ali McCaw. McCaw only used his beak to gnaw rawhide bones and try to bite guests so he'd been rubber-banded shut. Now that parrot couldn't croak out, "Jail Bait," or "Bite my balls," or other such he'd learned during a hard life. How he landed in the San Soon, sharing a cage with a false wisteria tree so covered in dust few knew what it was, was a mystery. Everyone but Ti-Jean was afraid to go in there, and Ti only did when he was drunk: but it worked out that Ti was drunk daily so McCaw got fed regular. Ti-Jean'd curse that Ali like two sailors sharing a poop deck. He'd grab that drooping dust tree and shake it till the fuzz flew. That parrot'd scream, "Bust my butt!" and Ti'd answer, "You kiss my ass." We girls would giggle and duck down behind the front counter awaiting Buster to run into the lobby, thin neck craning in his collar, cheeks flushing high under his eyes, saying, "What's this? What's this?" in his nervous wimpy way.

"You want to come in here to clean?" Ti'd swing the door back in invitation as Ali'd sling himself upside down and sideways, all his colored feathers ruffling, his little eyes mean and red, and say, "Lift my leg, love." Buster'd blush and back off.

Now here they come. Ti-Jean, though drunk, looks nice in the pirate getup they fixed for him; a patch that makes him walk slightly crookedy goes well with his natural list. Ali has his claws wrapped in baby booties and he's being pushed along on a metal IV stand that Creighton got from the hospital when he worked the emergency ward. Ali tries hard to spit some nastiness out, but the rubber band holds. The most he can do is hang upside down and look bored, but that parrot has a sense of drama. He pulls up smartly and sits and flares out his wings like red sails. Ti flinches.

Now here comes the kitchen staff, and the wrangles over which would come first—the dining room girls or the kitchen girls— was something. Finally it was decided: kitchen first, then back to the kitchen to fix the feast, then the Singing Chef yodeling tunes from *Oliver*, then dining girls back to bring out the food, now fixed, and last the waiters, led by George because they were gonna sing their Gullah tune. No one knew the words but them, and others who lived out South Island, but it must have been a good one because everyone who did know that deep blue husky tongue laughed a lot. Some fell right to the floor getting tickled over words like *jujullalla.*

Here's Orleen, without a grain of sense, striking up on "Born Free" as Lotte led in the kitchen group, she dignified in a pure white cotton wraparound against her eggplant black. She looked at Orleen like she'd kill and that stupid music maker segues into "The Candy Man," which didn't sit well either, Lotte's boy Candy having been put back into the penitentiary for 5 to 10 for pulling firearms in a convenience store. The food staff followed Lotte's steps and she took them big and steady, canceling that music to slow like it was on the wrong speed. Only Janie, from the sauce table, head tied up in a bright blue rag, and Creighton with his hospital turquoise shower cap shoved back showed the least musicality, picking up their feet and prancing in place. The Bread men wear white caps low and sinister and stare straight ahead.

Then come the dining hostess Marsha and her sidekick, the salad mistress, LaMona, both in sequinned specs, see-through platform shoes, and dresses for the statuesque. In the Cockle Shell you sat where Marsha told you to sit and ate that salad with egg dive-bombed on it that LaMona made or you'd know what for. You might end up like that kitten they'd taken home and stepped on, accidentally they said. Those four black eyes, rhinestone rimmed, filled up with tears that didn't run their mascara. None of us under ninety pounds trusted them. LaMona was always getting her fingers caught in the ironing board so that the hands that made your salad had Band-Aids in varying degrees of dirtiness all over them.

Now here comes the Chef. All ranks turn and salute with right hands raised in a Heil Hitler stance.

"Ah, what?" he chortles in a lissome way.

"A song," we straggle back.

Dub has his left hand up instead of his right and a lot of the

A Small Hotel

Swan Scouts are changing right to left. I can't ever tell which is which either unless I got a writer's bump or a hurt hangnail.

"A song," the Chef gurgles again, sweeping his high hat off and on.

Chef Lonny is well liked and sings good, just a little too near and too loud for most folks who are eating. It's upsetting to suddenly hear, one inch from your ear, "Food—glorious food." That's enough to make you jump like Jell-O.

Gay Lee's supposed to sing "More Please" to start things off, but she's shy. Her only sound ever has been on the flute, so her words are wisped off on the wind. Chef Lonny gapes for his cue, so Hobie shouts strong, "More Damn Please!" We all sway, smacking our lips over porridge and holding out our hands as bowls like Ms. Cleta choreographed; the Swan Scouts look like teasing muggers to me. The wind is beginning to blow and the waves run in, dip dap dapping on the sand and climbing up the hill. Orleen ends the song with a wail of the organ that tops Chef Lonny's own. The guests clap their palms in an anxious patter. A few are thinking of sneaking off, but Officer Swan has blocked the getaways. They'd have to wade right through the baby pool.

Now the parade is coming to an end with Bertie and his two helpers, neither of which I'd ever seen before, but this is typical of the garden crew. One day of pushing a hand mower around fifty acres of tall island grass, being screeched at by Ms. Cleta not to cut the viburnum down, you never saw them again. These two look pale, so they probably came from the pen. One snaps his clippers fast in time to Orleen's tune, wriggling his face, pulling it up on one side, down on the other, and pooching his mouth out in a circle, and in general making everyone on the front row nervous. Bertie pushes the hand mower and it click clack click clacks, rick rack rick racks. The other guy has a green hose looped around his shoulder like an epaulet. Every now and then he makes his mean mouth into a square grin. Bertie plods like he always does, looking up with sweat running down his face, like he makes you feel sorry for him outside every day.

Orleen plays "Greensleeves" and scoots around on the organ bench, lifting up her head to look over the edge to bring attention to her cleverness. She's a sequinned specs age too, but wears a brocade Chinese dress that shows she has those skinny legs that are the last to go when everything else has cut and run. She has on golden platform shoes and her heel bounces in rhythm. When she gets going she bends double on herself and is the nearest thing to an organ bench pad you ever saw. Her hair is yellow and loose and she pitches it back to stand crouch-kneed and wag her rear and get expressive. There is applause for her choices and she beams; her two eyeteeth pick up the light.

Orleen wants to go to Atlanta and audition to play organ for the Braves. "I'd be great at that," she says. "I would. You got to have brains to think up connections, you got to have a repertoire and you have to be fast."

Now we are all swaying and singing in various ways the world in harmony and the men do their hmmmmms as we march smartly back into the hotel. The acts start out with Buster dressed like a clown. He does some funny turns. I don't watch much because I'm in the corner going over in my mind all the possible dive combinations anyone could ever call. Buster has on a curly rainbow wig and a big red nose and for once his eyes look separate, perched on either side of that round apple. His falls off the low board when he lurches in his chicken feet are getting howls from the crowd. I hear the first shot fired by a sheriff at bay.

"They're starting to shoot for the stars," Ms. Cleta says.

But whatever it was that Buster did last struck a chord with everyone. They are screeching out there and Lotte, eye peering onto the pool, says, "Shame, shame." George and Creighton are laughing and Hobie's not talking quite so smooth, so I know it's some kind of dirty stuff that Buster's got into. Ms. Cleta, however, seems to be taking it well. She joins him at poolside, where he moves into a funny song and makes eyes around his nose at her. She blushes as deep a color as her dress. In general, Buster acts so jolly and unlike himself that I can see what drew a person like Ms. Cleta to link her fortunes with a man who thinks string ties are a fashion peak.

Marsha and LaMona rush by with trays of drinks. "They've taken in over $500 in bar orders," LaMona breathlessly says, then over her shoulder, "They're running out of food."

If this were any ordinary day someone would be in Buster's red pickup truck that says "Buster Coombs/His Hotel" and has a picture of the San Soon painted on the side, making a run to Jacksonville to make a deal on discount bananas from a docked ship, or on crates of potato chips from anyone who had them.

Now it's time. Hobie's introducing us. He's holding our hands above our heads and I'm smiling, my face cracking; my eyelashes feel like little spider legs and my mouth like a candle. When Hobie says, "Do you want to say anything?" I say, "Yes. May the best *woman* win, and all you females bet on me!"

"Yippee!" yell Gay Lee, LaMona, Marsha, my mamma, Ms. Cleta, and most of the jazz dancers, who are sitting in pretzel-like shapes showing off their turnout.

Greg says, "Can the boys win!" Which gets him yells too, mostly from the sheriffs, who are as dumb as he is.

"That's the spirit," shouts Buster. "The age-old battle." He grabs Ms. Cleta and kisses her. She doesn't seem to mind. Then Greg grabs me and kisses me and I do mind. I say funny and fast, "Puleeease . . ." and everyone laughs.

Then the lights around the pool flicker on and the interior lights of the pool change color and the whole thing is glowing. We draw straws from Hobie's hand and Greg goes first. Ms. Cleta has the mike and she's explaining how they did this contest in Atlanta. You can see this crowd doesn't want to be bested so they are already shouting out stunts as she tries to calm them down, saying, "It's only dives they're doing, nothing else." Then they start to shout out outrageous dives.

Greg says, "Listen to that. I couldn't do that, could you, Deenie?"

I am above it all, I am a circus trapeze flyer, I am trembling. I can hardly wait to start. The baby pool is full of folks in evening clothes, sitting there totally wet and smiling. Now Orleen begins to play and the contest begins.

The first few practice dives I hardly remember. I'm waiting in line shivering, dripping wet, and my heinie's hanging out of my suit. A light warm rain is starting to fall, but the guests have really got with it now. They are throwing all sorts of money into the pool and the sheriffs up on the Hacienda roof are hurling off strap lawn chairs into the courtyard, and occasionally shooting off a highway flare or rocket into the night sky. Everybody is placing bets and Creighton is in his element, collecting and doubling them. Orleen is hard-pressed to keep up; she starts "Red Sails in the Sunset" in triple time.

They are shouting out the wildest dives: triple gainer, double loop twist, jackknife half combination. Greg has executed a perfect backflip twist which he made up in the air, arched himself beautifully in this odd light made up of pearly moon and pale blue lanterns that flicker around the pool, shine into its depth. It seems a sea of sky that I'll dive into.

The board still reverberates from his dive as the guests roar and clap. Then his head breaks surface, water pouring down his face, creasing his hair in a perfect center part. The guys yell, "More," begin to chant.

I'm goosebumped all over; for the first time in my life I have nipples. Hobie takes my damp smock as I begin to mount the

A Small Hotel

ladder. Greg hauls himself to the side of the pool, shaking water from his ears, grin splitting his face. He is so happy I almost feel like grinning back. My toes grip the wet metal rung, slippery, treacherous, the first test. I will do a perfect whatever it is that they'll call. On the third step my ankle is braceleted by Hobie's hand. He's as close to loving me as he'll ever be. He squeezes my ankle. "Anything is possible," he says, then gives my heel a take-five slap.

The board trembles with my run, my fast stops, my feints into the air. I make the crowd gasp with my daring, make Greg look worried. As I begin this last long run to leap high into the air, I hope that they will call out, "Swan," so I can fly.

La Plume de Ma Tante

I can top that," Betty says, leaning forward to shake out a Salem and light it with a kitchen match. "I was one of the proofreaders for the New York City telephone book." She jerks her feet to the coffee table, drumming bare heels till her ankle bracelet jingles. "That was the damndest job."

"Do you want another drink?" Jerry calls from the kitchen. "What job are you telling about? That one where the kid stabbed people with a fork?"

"No. Crissley, Pride & Wells, and yes, a fruit punch with rum." My aunt leans back to begin telling me about her job. I'm unemployed and pregnant but at least I'm married; Steve has a B.A. and is getting interviews.

In 1967 when the shipyards in Norfolk closed down a while my Uncle Jerry lost his job. He did something undisclosed with the nuclears. He and Betty moved to Washington, D.C., and lived on the highway between Falls Church and a planned community being built while Jerry went to Walter Reed to have the chips in his arm checked out. Some sucker'd smacked him on the funny bone during the Korean war and his arm always hung strange after that. So while he collected various government checks for being out of work, looking for work, and having had to work, Aunt Betty got a job.

"Crissley, Pride & Wells—I know they made those names up," she says. "And when I think of what we had to do . . ." She fans herself with her hand. Betty is in her mid-forties, a purple-hennaed redhead who always wears false eyelashes, always has long

La Plume de Ma Tante

nails. When decals came in she wore butterflies on her thumbs. She still wears her high school ring, sapphire with *Sic Semper Fidelis*. The D.C. area is expensive and they needed bucks but fast, so when she saw the ad for proofreaders, $95 for the week and no experience needed, she jumped. Since it was only for a week she knew they'd never check references. "Never do if it's just a little job." She grabbed a red pen and drove to the quonset hut that C.P. & W. called home.

"Should have known the minute I found out that Crissley was a Mormon with ten kids what we were in for, but you know me." In my family Betty and her sisters Coy and Hazel Marie were daredevils who'd try anything. One of them trained wild tigers for commercials and the other once played a hooker on "Hill Street Blues." Uncle Jerry brings in the second round of drinks. He's opened up a pack of Mallomars.

"Ugh." Betty scoots them off the tray with her toe. "I think you're doing dope again."

"I'm not." His tone is wounded, his face suspiciously serene. Jerry was always runner-up to Most Handsome in high school and his face is described by some as sweet, by others as too dished-in. There is debate in the family over whether his chin dimple is too deep. His younger brother Sampy, who looks enough like him to be his twin, is a hairstylist in Portallis who has been known to bleach his hair and has the self-conscious style of a guy who vaguely resembles Kirk Douglas.

"Imagine if you will . . ." Betty says, determined to make us see this job.

We've been staying with my aunt and uncle this past week while my husband waits to hear if he'll be hired by anyone he talked to in the last go-round. Each time Steve drags in wilted with his tales of woe Betty and Jerry try to cheer him up. Certainly, at this time I don't seem to be doing him a bit of good, having been told to restrict my salt and stay off my feet. Most of this visit I've spent crunching ice by the poolside or catching up on the *Reader's Digest*.

"A room with no windows," Betty continues. "Nothing but textured walls and ceiling tiles that look like pigskin painted white. Tables down each side, and fluorescent light, and two persons to each table and six tables to a side. At the front another big old table with boxes marked *rough* and *proof* and *checked* and *done* and another box of bright red pens. That . . ." She pauses to exhale, roll her head into the smoke, reinhaling it. ". . . is the setting for this tale of hell."

Steve is slumped over on the hassock pushing his socks down between his toes. My uncle pops an entire Mallomar into his mouth sideways. "It started off fine at first," she says, "like a first day of school with a nice teacher, Mr. Crissley, dressed in navy—soft voice, sweet smile, willing to explain." She sits at attention now, knees together and face bright, prim and ready for the term. "We got supplies. A sheet that was clear plastic and had proofreader's signs and a see-through ruler that had its end magnified and five red felt-tip pens." Their job, she explains, was to proofread the New York City telephone book, all five boroughs beginning with the Bronx.

"Why the Bronx?" I ask.

Steve lifts his head and I know why. He'd read somewhere that words that end with an *x* strike people as sinister. He woke me one night when we'd been married about six months to tell me this news. We spent some time trying to prove the theory true. Sex, we'd decided, could go both ways.

"Honey, a company in New York hadn't done the job right, so C. P. & W. had taken on the Bronx book to show that city crew what we—those hired folks sitting in D.C. on that gray day—could do to show New Yorkers up."

Jerry washes down his Mallomar with glugs of Pearl, then

says, "You told them yet about that boy who never did them right, but raced his ruler down the page to put a red check at the bottom?"

"No, damnit, but you just did!" Betty jumps up and slaps him on the head. His second cookie leaps from his mouth. He sputters and laughs.

"Forget you heard that," she says. "Jerry never sets a story up right. You have to know the boy in question had the head of someone who would do such a thing. Forehead sloped back into one long continuing wave of hair. Eyebrows that wanted to get together, and a name to fit that scruffiness. I can't recall it at the moment. That jerk—first he coughed every time anyone smoked." Betty doubles over, looking pained. "Then that brat complained, and because he was proofing so fast he was listened to. After that, if we wanted to smoke, and I wasn't the only one who did . . ." She pauses, looks defiantly at Jerry, who does not smoke—more sheepishly at Steve, who used to smoke but stopped—lights a new cigarette off the butt end, stubs the old one out, and makes a face.

"Smokers had to get up and go out of the room, and we lost pages that way. You got extra money after a certain number of pages because they gave you points. Had to finish a quota of at least ten a day, and that was manageable, but more than that you had to push it. Then he got permission to play the radio." Betty jerks her head in little nods to her chest; her hair moves in one piece like a helmet. "I'll never forget '96 Tears.'" Screwing up her mouth, she howls, "Cry, cry, cry!" Then she sits bolt up. "And all the time that little creep was cheating. When I think of the awful music that I was forced to listen to . . ."

"How did you catch on?" Steve is slightly drunk now because Uncle Jerry's hand is heavy. He's got a grin I recognize as his bemused-at-human-nature stance. He was a philosophy major and matters of reason and logic pick at him.

"Oh," Betty says, "it didn't take long because C. P. & W. spot-checked the work, of course, as those of us who were older and worked before knew. Still, I'd have never had the nerve." Sipping iced tea, I imagine a brash and nervy boy in handcuffs being led away, his hands red-stained with proofing ink, his eyes abnormally shifty.

"Yeah," she muses, "it started off fun. A bunch of us, about ten, grandfathers and college girls and ordinary people like me, all with red pens and long white shining sheets of paper filled with rows and rows of the teensiest names. At first everyone was laughing and yelling out, 'Listen to this—Ima Love, B. O. Crutch.' Then we'd all shriek. Hoped, as we did our list, to come across a really good name or a funny one. One time this girl from Roanoke found four on one page that had to do with death, and she was spooked all day." Betty draws her shoulders up and rounds her eyes. I try to think of four names I've known that have to do with the subject, but can only recall one girl named Toombs.

"But soon, very soon, about the middle of that first day, after a provided lunch, which was dried-out sandwiches and Kool-Aid in paper cups, each one of us began to realize that for one solid week we'd be together in this white room that smelled like olive loaf, looking at this smaller-than-a-phone-book's print." She breathes deep, exhales. "I'll tell you, by then not even the most wonderful name . . . and some of them . . . Alejandro CaraSara-Maldonado of 57 Fox Street in the Bronx? Could you ever match that name? When I first read it I could see him walk out of his house, all swimming black eyes and a yellow shirt." She is dreaming of this swarthy lover; her shoulders sway.

"Probably pushing dope," Jerry says. She shoos him away.

"Once I knew someone named Pheralyn Dove. And another girl named Primrose Noble," I say.

Betty wags her head in a gesture of pretty-good-but-just-you-wait. "All we hoped for," she says, "was that some name like Brown or Jones or Smith was down the line. Because, see, at first you wanted mistakes and then you didn't. You were afraid if there weren't any mistakes on your page you'd missed them. So you went back checking. It was the perfect job for a neurotic, or maybe a person who thinks they're perfect."

My aunt has stiffened her face so that she is at once precise and shaky. "One time, after hours of I don't know what they were, *Krz*'s that ended with *skz*'s, I wanted some plain Robert Harrises. There were rows of them waiting in the box when that fast brat—why can't I get his name?—ran up and got them instead of me. I was so mad I felt like dumping Johnson to Keenen on the floor. He managed to avoid the Smiths too!"

"He'd been fired by that time," Jerry added.

"I'd hoped he was. Now, on the third day those of us who were left (it's remarkable how we dwindled to the desperate) only said a name if it was real unusual, like the whole thing went together. Seven 7's in the address and the name was El Ak El El El or Huffy Puffy Bofaba." She looks to see if I'm paying attention.

"Those aren't real," I say.

"Oh no? Why in the world would I make up names like that?" She shoves my leg with her foot. "By that Wednesday you'd only get a murmur of appreciation for being alive. Meanwhile, that kid's music slamming into your ears, and having to get up and go out to the bathroom to smoke, and not allowed to have water or anything to drink because you might spill it on the precious Moynahans of the Grand Concourse. We six who were left almost reached a point of rebellion." Betty rears up and fists her hands. She silently mouths "Death to the Shah" and shakes her shoulders. "There was a lot of loud shoe-shuffling going on under the table and a lot of filching of red pens. See, the tips went flat and smeared like Merthiolate. It was enough to make you sick. Make you want to leave a big fat blotch when you corrected something."

"She'd come home every night with a splitting headache, a heart full of hate, and personal gossip about Crissley." Jerry massages Betty's shoulder in memory.

"That weasel brat and the girl from Roanoke . . ." Betty says.

The Purchase of Order

"She was the kind of blonde that sucks on the ends of her hair. Knew one of Crissley's many kids and he was said to have a way with women besides his wife, like Mormons often do. One of his women had got him and Pride and Wells into this telephone adventure. The next thing we were warned about was that C. P. & W. would try and rope us into some kind of history document project for the feds."

"Probably the prison rolls," Steve adds. He's had four beers and two and a half grasshopper-margarita combinations and three Mallomars. Chocolate icing browns his lips, but around the eyes he looks somewhat green.

"Now came Thursday," Betty says, "and I was counting the days of not having to watch the weasel ever again, because by that time you knew everybody well. Think of living for a solid week on a Greyhound with the same bunch, but you never get off." Then she shoots up, shouting, "Brad Scotella! That's his name."

She becomes Brad and, knees bent bare and bony, scuttles around the coffee table, holding her cigarette like a pen. "He was a key jingler, a Navy windbreaker wearer, and I watched him run his eye down the Meyer to Meyerowitz like a racing form, check his red X, plop it down in the in-box, and grab something easy like Miller, leaving all the Muellers with their odd e's to us. But then on Thursday afternoon . . ." She is entering the doorway of the lost room, head craned for Brad, ear set for his music. "He was gone. And we started seeing in the to-be-dones all his finished sheets with red streaks down the side where he'd liked to show his fast eye. Yeah, his cheating was caught in a spot-check. This national treasure . . ." Her tone is sarcastic. "This human computer, this spoiler of days of people like me worrying about their lack of education . . ." Her voice rises. "He hadn't done a single thing he was supposed to."

"Calm down, honey." Jerry pats her instep. "They asked you to stay on, didn't they?"

La Plume de Ma Tante

"Yes," she says, "and I was almost dumb enough to say yes." She swivels her head, pleading with the appreciation plaques hung on the wall to refute her past weakening. "They said they'd keep only the college degrees and I didn't have one, *or* those who showed themselves 'particularly competent.' When I was coming up . . ." Betty looks directly at Steve now, he's the educated one. I'm pregnant and so don't exactly count because a college degree didn't help me to stay out of trouble; might as well have gone to beauty school. She discounts me now. "When I was coming up you didn't have to have a degree. Only if you loved to learn or wanted to waste time. I'd found my man in high school, so I didn't need to go and hunt." She and Jerry fell in love when they were fifteen and their bedroom dressers are covered with pictures of them at the Snowball and the Senior Prom. "So I was flattered that I was considered good, but then I sobered up and thought, what in the world are you thinking of; you're not even up to Smith yet. Then I thought of all the Tuckers, the Weinbergs, and the Zinns to come, and shook my head no thanks, took my check, and ran."

Jerry says, "Whole damn business went kablooie the next year, we heard." He is putting a stack of records on so we can dance. Every night of the week we've been here we've done something: shot pool in the Clubhouse, played Pee Wee golf, or bowled at the Carlton Lanes. When we get home and before bed Jerry always says, "Anybody want to dance?"

"You had to keep the same five red pens," Betty says. She fishes orange slices out of her drink. She is still baffled. "Felt tips get all flattened out. You can't make good corrections with a flat pen, and they didn't give us any new ones after Wednesday."

"Let's dance, honey." Jerry pulls her up to move to the sound of Nat King Cole singing "Dance, Ballerina, Dance."

My aunt and uncle own nothing but each other and their lives, though once they had a chihuahua named Tippy who could squeeze himself into a coffee cup, but he died of excessive shivering when they lived in Maine. All my life whenever I visited them they lived somewhere different in someplace new: a trailer, a studio condo, once a live-in motel shaped like a teepee. They had their travels and all their various jobs and they'd tried to have kids but couldn't. When Betty saw me filling up her apartment door with my seersuckered belly, she grabbed me to her, kissed my face, and murmured, "Oh baby, baby mine." They live on the second floor of La Cienta condos where they rent, and though from this apartment they can't see the pool, there are reflected lights from water, blue and green, and a false tropic smell of chlorine on concrete that puts you in mind of holidays and Mexico. On their balcony is a sign prohibiting more than six adults of normal size, along with a grill and two lawn chairs. Jerry and Betty keep their no-speed bikes chained to the avocado tree they bought off a guy who moved to Tucson. Voices from the pool rise up muffled, seeming sometimes desperate, sometimes fun.

I dance too, my teeth on Steve's shirt collar, stretching it out like a Greek handkerchief. My aunt reaches out to pat me and we four touch hands, dance all in a line. "Remind me, honey," she says, "to tell you about working in a funny old hotel."

The Purchase of Order

Lou Maxey is hanging over the top of the seat, her behind a likely target. She's slipped her pink plastic shoes half off and they dangle like loose skin. There are rustling sounds from the back.

"What in the hell are you doing?" Marlon asks, pushing in the cigarette lighter, which he has to lean around her in order to do.

"I'm looking for that package of Cheese Nuggets I packed in here. I'm hungry."

"We just had breakfast less than an hour ago," he says around his light-up. "You had the Trencherman. You couldn't be hungry."

She looks back over her shoulder, tries to lift her foot up and sideways to jog his knee; it's impossible, so she bumps his shoulder with her rear. "How do you know? You're not me. And I'm hungry."

Lou is one of those little women who never look any older than about sixteen until you're close up. Her hair is crisp and close and dark and her eyes are the brown of spaniels'. She's had five kids, four in the first six years of marriage, and then a decade's wait before her baby Jason, now in the Navy on a ship anchored off Greece. Lou likes to think of her baby in the Mediterranean, near the place and the myth he was named for, and how apt the name she chose. Although there are lots of Jasons now, there weren't many then, and her boy, with his curly golden hair, thick and spongy as sheep wool on his arms and chest, was like a fleecy thing. "It looks like Santa's beard's on his legs," a little cousin said once at the beach.

You could never imagine your own children making love, Lou thought. She could never imagine anyone making love, but she could picture a dark Grecian girl with red ribbons in her hair cradling against Jason's chest. Marlon's body hair was different. It was rusty and tufty with a strange patch on the left chest. He had smooth upper arms that were furred like pelts from elbow to wrist. Everything about the man amazed her, and they'd been married almost thirty years.

Last night at the motel while she watched *The Sting* on TV, Marlon, feet crossed precisely one on top of the other in a wedge, read the local paper, which he always did wherever they stopped. "Guess who this sounds like," he said, reading a letter to the editor from a man who complained about the sewer lines, the garbage pick-up, and the planting of iris bulbs in front of City Hall. "'And in conclusion . . .'" Marlon pulled the sentence out. "'City Council should get going or get out.'"

Lou, who'd only half-listened from the second tirade on, said, "That's your mamma all over, Marlon."

He smiled, shook the paper back into creases, and settled in to reading the classifieds while she got up, one eye on the TV show, and wandered over to the window, which was oddly high, partly blocked by an air-conditioning unit.

"'Two bedroom house for $195,'" Marlon read. "That's not bad." She mmmed that she heard, but mainly was looking for something, anything previous guests might have left behind. Once she'd found a bookmark, navy leather stamped with gold designs, tucked into the Gideon. Another time a little girl's hair-bow, fashioned into a rose with a frill of plastic lace. Lou collected such things as souvenirs. She liked to own matchbooks that she found under beds in which she and many others had slept.

Marlon had finished reading, was watching the movie with a bemused expression.

"What part's that?" She bent over him and without a word he flipped her over on her back and splattered his mouth against her stomach. She pushed at his head, saying, "Don't, no, stop,

The Purchase of Order

don't you dare," and then Marlon went from splatting to pink belly, and while she giggled and shoved him away, shouting for Robert Redford to save her, she was excited by the sound of his hands patting her stomach, moving fast up and down her flesh.

This summer's trip is following a pattern set ten years ago. The Maxeys hop into their van aiming to just go. That first day when Marlon drove it home, Lou walked around and around it, thinking it was as big as a bus. Marlon scraped off the manufacturer's name, KING OF THE ROAD, saying, "That makes me sick. I'll choose my own name." Then he left the space bare, tacky with a residue of stickiness that collects insects and dust. A decade later KI and RD still show like lines in the wax of a magic slate.

This summer, like all before, they'll travel anywhere and everywhere they want, not a plan in their heads, except to follow their own feelings. "What will be, will be" is the Maxeys' motto on these trips, but truth to tell, Lou does worry and marks the maps and schedules the stops so they ca i visit with all their kids and grandchildren. After Labor Day, when families leave the road to see to purchases of new notebooks and underwear, they turn back too, clean up their van, and park it to the side of the bungalow near Austin where they've decided to spend the rest of their lives.

Lou calls her friends, goes to the YWCA for her Jane Fonda exercise class, and twice weekly puts on her crinolines and she and Marlon go to the Square Dance Club. "No ties, not even string ones" was the deal before he'd go. She loves the way he looks standing across from her in the square, wearing his plaid blue shirt with pearl buttons, open at the collar, jeans turned up in a pale roll, and boots, cut-under heels marking up the gym floor. When the caller does his do-si-do, Marlon moves his nose sideways, lets his eyelids droop in a criminal manner, and swings circle-box-circle until she's his, caught at the waist. Even when these evenings make her ache and soak her feet, see them peel in a pan of Epsom salts, she loves it. She feels exactly as she did when she first met Marlon, then married him, against everybody's will.

Early in their marriage, when he'd lost his job, the one he quit high school for, a restlessness set in in him. She'd be at work, a half-day job her daddy got her at a plate glass company doing bills, and in the afternoons stuffing burgers into bags, when she's look up to catch Marlon whisking out of sight. Sometimes, later in the day, he'd come to get a roast beef that had got cold. "Can't stick around," he'd say. "Got to see a man."

Sometimes he'd borrow a dollar, or pat her on the belly where the baby now was. They didn't talk much about the baby; somehow she knew it made Marlon too sad. Only at night in bed in the trailer, where the neighbors slammed their glass louvered doors so hard the foundation shook, Lou'd scoot up against him, feeling the swell of their baby between, and she knew how Marlon felt. "Wasn't supposed to be this way," he whispered, turning to embrace her. The baby's bulk pushed him to the wall as she felt the corners of her mouth tingling at the touch of his lips.

Near when the baby was due Lou began to worry about what would happen, how they'd work things out. She'd catch herself sitting at her desk at Mitchell's Glass having stapled the same bill twice. She found it harder and harder to force a smile for customers. The smell of onion and grease at her afternoon job seemed never to leave her. She was constantly figuring out schedules, adding sums in her head even as she sprinkled grated cheese on the taco special.

"I've got a job," Marlon told her when he popped up at the Burger 52 one day right after lunch and was persuaded to sit down and have a cherry coke and onion rings. Everyone liked Marlon. He was even-tempered, told good stories, and he worked hard: it's just there had to be work to do.

"Where is this job?" asked the other hop, whose boyfriend had got the boot a few weeks before Marlon. "In Alaska?"

The Purchase of Order

Marlon looked up, winked, held an onion like a ring over his finger and said, "Yes." Everyone laughed but Lou; she knew Marlon never kidded about change. He ate that ring, finished his coke, and, pointing his finger at her like a gun, said, "Later."

That's how they ended up in a van with a three-week-old baby girl and some household goods, driving to this promised land where Marlon worked construction and Lou watched babies, her own among them, and all they made went for food and rent. The sunsets hung red for hours, it seemed, teasing them with the thought of dark, and Marlon wasn't happy. Evenings he'd sit in front of the television after the baby was in bed and hold his knees, shoving the heel of his hand like gunning a car, fast, faster, staring straight ahead and clenching his jaws.

One night when he came home Lou was nursing the baby, both curled up in a corner of the couch. He sat down on the coffee table facing her, clasping his hands like being good at school; then he leaned his chin against his steepled thumbs.

"Do you want me to rub your neck?" she asked.

He raised his head and his eyes looked swimmy, even though he was smiling. "I've got another job, babe. On the coast, doing something. Don't know what, but I'll guarantee you it'll be dirty and dangerous." He tapped Lou's chin with his fist, gently pulled the baby's hair. Lou was pregnant again, bigger this time, with things going strange. Her ankles swelled straight to her knees, turning white and crackly like old china plates. Marlon would pop her toes at night, rub warmth into her feet with his hands, which were small for a man's.

They never stopped making love, even when it seemed that everything they did or didn't do led to babies. Their second was born in Louisiana, then another boy in Tampa, then a baby girl born on their way from Arizona to Alabama, and Lou's chief memory of those years is of trying to keep her babies clean, keep them up off floors where who-knew-what had gone on. They lived on a live-in ship, in a one-room kitchenette on the third floor of a beach hotel, and once—she doesn't like to think of it—in the back part of a converted van. Some rainy days during that bad time she would gather her children around to sleep huddled like puppies. They saw a lot of places, and Marlon's excitement about them kept her going.

"Living in a place is not the same as visiting it," he'd said, "because while you get to know the towns better, you know them less." Lou thought that was true. Places were like relatives: somehow the longer you knew one, the less you valued it. Moving off and then coming back for visits let you see all the sweetnesses. She'd picked up Marlon's rhythm by this time and wondered as she wrapped her cups in the Sunday comics, readying for another move, if she could ever go back to one place. She'd met a woman who'd shopped at the same Piggly Wiggly all her life, and Lou marveled at that.

Sometimes the places where they had lived blended into each other, all seeming a dream that held these constants: a laundromat, a convenience store, and a drive-in on the edge of town where she and Marlon would get out to sit on a blanket spread in front of the grille while the children slept on in the back seat, the speakers turned low for their ears. Then sometimes Lou would be struck with a recall of a place so vivid that she thought, If I went back there now, I could find my way around. Sometimes at night, when she couldn't sleep, she played a game with herself. She picked a town they'd lived in and drove around in it in her head. When Marlon heard her muttering, "Turn left for the Dixie Pig," he'd sleepily ask, "Where are you?"

Getting used to change is easy for her now, but it wasn't always. She's happy to think she can adjust, move from place to place, seek out the stores, the banks, and the schools. She liked to get the family settled in and clear a place on the refrigerator for the kids' school work while Marlon went off to all the different jobs that he had.

The Purchase of Order

Whenever she went back to the town Marlon came from she saw the same people walking down the same streets. They'd die in the same frame houses they lived in, she thought. Then she wanted to get in the car and go, drive away with Marlon and the kids to somewhere they'd never lived before.

Each year when they start their trip they have a purpose. It is one that has never been taken out and examined, one that is rarely discussed except in memories that come up—a purpose neither of them really knows how to explain. What moves these summers for the Maxeys is a search that has shaped their lives for the last decade: they are looking for a family they once knew, without whose presence everything in life has been more pale, a family they've continued to think about and talk about. Lamont and Jean Dillon and their kids—when they met them twenty-two years ago in Arkansas, it was one of those meetings between two families where everything hits right and it is forever and always. But in this case, the Maxeys don't know how, it fell away through not keeping in touch, both of them moving on too many times.

When Lou wants to make an event memorable, she ransacks her brain for recollections of the Dillons, especially Lamont in his boneless height. "How he keeps his pants up is a mystery, and I'm married to the man," Jean said, rolling her eyes, always in a laugh putting her left hand up to cover where a tooth was gone, another gone gray. Lamont's back seam fell flat between his thighs.

At various times over the years when Lou has helped her children learn to cut meat, do a chain stitch in crochet, or print between the lines, she's seen Lamont's hands as they shaped a little figure with his knife. Concentrating as solemnly as the child who stood waiting to see what would emerge from between the wood and the blade, he'd roll the scrap of pine in his fingers and seem surprised himself to see it become a donkey or a tiny dancing man. He'd lift up his head and his thick eyebrows, under which his eyes, so light a blue they were almost white, were innocent, and smile a fool's smile, the corners of his mouth pulling up into his cheeks.

"Now lookee here," he'd murmur, balancing the figure in the well of his outstretched hand. "Let me take my payment." The knife blade quickly cut the thinnest lock from the edge of the child's hair; the blade tip near their ears made the older ones shiver, the little ones giggle. "This here's magic hair," he'd say. "Have to add it to my pile."

"If he'd ever get money for those carvings we'd have a dozen pillows stuffed with duck fuzz down, if we wanted them," Jean would complain, then light a Tareyton, pulling in smoke, the cigarette moving from the center of her lip like a dowser's rod in the strength of her inhale. When she wanted to be funny she'd cross her eyes before blowing out the match.

That day in the laundromat Lou couldn't have known that Jean would be any other than the kind of friend you usually make there who helps you fold. Even though Marlon was good with the kids, Lou always took her brood with her; too many things can happen in a trailer court on an off-day when men, in work or out, are drinking beer and fixing cars. One guy with a saucer scar on his shoulder scared the kids by popping out his top three teeth and clanking them up and down. At the laundromat Lou would sit her four down, give them Chocolate Soldiers and Nabs, and buy each of them a comic book. Later, during Dry, Marlon would come to help fold. Sometimes he'd wrap himself like an Arab in a sheet, dancing a mummy's dance, and make everybody in the long linoleumed room laugh.

That's how they first met, Jean with her pile of threadbare towels and striped Handi-Wipes she used for washrags—that's what she called them instead of washcloths—and all her kids, who made Lou's crazy. But she was such a good-natured lanky girl, so quick to smile at Marlon's silliness, so willing to let the children

The Purchase of Order

be lively in their romping around with peanut shell earrings clamped to their lobes, that Lou liked her right away.

Lou was folding diapers when all of a sudden this woman with hair yanked straight back and features looking forward began to help. "These sure are white," she said. "Why don't you use disposables?"

"Can't afford to," Lou answered, wanting to laugh and not knowing why, but knowing right then that this friendship, based from the beginning on knowing everything bad about each other's underwear, would last.

"Where ya'll staying?" she'd questioned Lou, having said she was Jean Dillon and with a wave of a hand, diaper flapping like a sailor's flag, pointed out her husband Lamont, who was loading a commercial machine with a jumble of goods from towels to blue jeans. Marlon was outside walking all the kids in formation on the parking lot, yelling made-up orders: "Walk on tippy-toes. Now stick out your tongues." The children collapsed on hot tar in giggling heaps.

"My bunch," Jean said, shooing them off, the other hand shaking out a Tareyton. "Maisie, Jasper, Gordon, Ceil, and Autumn Ann. Where'd you say?" she asked again.

Lou had no choice but to tell her. "We're out at Doakes." She didn't like to be there. It was a rough place. Too many people slept in during the day, and they weren't on the night shifts either.

"Not so good for kids." Jean tongued her cigarette to the side of her mouth, squinted her eyes, and began to fold. "No place to let them run their spirits out."

"I try to get over to the park each day," Lou said.

"Come live by us," Jean offered. "Looks funny from the street— Clark's Courts—but inside it's just the place for kids. I manage there. It's not free, but no more than you're paying at Doakes."

Lou didn't know what to say, looked up at Jean, her lank

brown hair wreathed with smoke, her bright blue eyes eager and hopeful. "I'll have to talk to my husband," she said, and right then Marlon burst through the door crying, "Save me. Save me! Please!" holding the plate glass shut against the force of all the sweaty screeching children, pushing and laughing and shoving and shouting out the different sweet treats they wanted. "Stay still!" He mashed a frog face on the glass. "Sit down like sombrero men with your knees drawed up and each and every one of you will get a Fudgsicle." Then he came and stood by Lou and asked, "Who's taking over my diaper duty?"

Jean laughed, then hailed Lamont, who'd been resting, back against the porthole of the big machine, head down, dreaming. "Lamont, come meet these people. I'm getting them to come and live by us."

When Lamont Dillon looked up and smiled, Lou's heart fled out of her and she, who'd never given love to any man but Marlon, knew she loved him; not in the way of Marlon, nor that of her brother who'd died in the war, and for whom she cried for years, waking sometimes in the night, face wet with tears from a dream that he was showing her how to hit a pitch, sock the tetherball and knock it back to him. No, somehow it was as though Lamont Dillon was her, or as if, had she been a man, she'd have been exactly like him. He sauntered toward them, tall, skinny with thick black hair and an eerie half-breed Indian look of dark skin and blue eyes, all of him moving bonelessly and gracefully as he slid his shower shoes along. Lou looked over at Marlon, standing even with Jean's height: both of them looked like lean alley cats, rusty and triangular, emitting energy as they stood. She felt a burning, as if had they joined hands in a ring they'd explode into flames.

"You're at the turpentine camp?" Lamont drawled. His voice was rumbling, deep, almost phony in its bass level.

Marlon was jazzed up; he was joking already as he answered yes.

The Purchase of Order

They moved into Clark's Courts and Lou began to watch Jean Dillon closely for clues on how she lived; usually she let her kids go as wild as her house and the yard. Her kitchen was the kind where a brush filled with hair sits right next to a stick of melted butter; Lou always washed her own cups there. Once when Lou'd spilled a can of corn, Jean said, "Here, let me help you," then proceeded to kick the kernels under the shelf's overhang. She was always saying her kids were up to no good, even as she passed their school pictures around, and they loved her the same way, interrupting as she read her *True Romance.* "What do you want, you dirty bum?" With a long arm she'd grab a boy and kiss him as he squirmed, protested, "Mamma, no." They asked for Nutty Buddy money or a dime for the picture show. Jean always gave it.

They couldn't scare her either. "See here—spiders," said Ceil, a bony-chested ten-year-old with harlequin glasses that were pearl-tipped. "Bet you'd be afraid to touch them," she challenged Jean, who pulled her face all to the center and said, "Oh yeah?" then mounted them on her fingers and displayed them like rings. "Here, kids, Popsicles," she'd shout, or "Root beer floats, every-one." Her children had cavities and scabbed elbows and greasy hair and grayed knees and were totally secure in their parents' love.

Autumn Ann was a foster baby who'd been given them by a cousin to keep for a weekend, then left for a lifetime. Jean lugged her three-year-old weight around, fat diaper perched on a hip, Autumn sagging back like a Siamese twin joined at the waist. "Autumn Ann's like an extra pair of hands, aren't you, honey?" she said, and the little girl reached out for the bananas that were collecting flies in the fruit bowl. That year they'd taken in a little boy named Traveling Apple, born and raised in a veggie commune; he'd turned orange from being fed too many carrots. "Look at this sweet Seville," Jean said, kissing his apricot face.

"He's got a suntan all right," Lamont said and cradled the baby on his chest, the man's neck showing red in a V, the rest of his torso wiry with each muscle as defined as a drawing under his skivvy shirt. "Sleep, little fellow, sleep," he crooned in that deep voice that hummed the air.

One night they danced out on the cracked concrete patio of the courts. Jean tucked her hands into Lamont's back pocket and he wrapped both arms around her shoulders and all the children came running up to hang from their waists and trouble them; they looked like a whirligig that spins, ribbons floating in a circle. Wedged between was Autumn Ann, fat face pressed against their thighs, baby foot on each of their insteps, making them stiff-legged as they box-stepped to "In the Still of the Night." "Sho do, sha debe do," Lamont sang, and Lou, holding her littlest on her lap, legs dangling into the pool, felt the baby's feet kick splashes on her shins. She felt like crying as she watched them dance to Lamont's music. All the kids were giggling, Lou's and Marlon's trying to get in. They insinuated their arms into the circling couple, dragging their feet, acting like flour sacks instead of kids. Lamont and Jean pretended not to notice, kept their eyes closed and looked extra gooey as they staggered this hoopskirt of children around. Marlon sat down beside Lou, put his arm around her, and rubbed the baby's foot. "Why is it," he said, "life makes people so good and treats them so bad?" Lou buried her head in his neck, smelling chlorine on him, loving him as she felt the baby squirm and wiggle to get free.

So on this trip, like all the others since they began their quest, Lou and Marlon followed the fairs and flea markets and asked in each town where it was that people might raise goats or lots of kids, and always got a laugh. They'd gone to each town in a Louisiana parish Lamont once mentioned he lived in, asking if anyone knew them, knew a fine mechanic, a wood-carver named Dillon, and got no answer but no.

On the third week out they decided to lift their spirits by look-

The Purchase of Order

ing for barbecue. Here on the edge of a Louisiana town they saw a place that was exactly what you looked for when you were hungry for good barbecue: a wood shack, discolored by smoke and redolence rising out of the wood, the sky perfumed with the odor of wood chips and vinegar and crisp roasting, and in the yard off to the side, a lean-to with tables and little children climbing on them.

"Let's stop here," Marlon said, pulling in. When they got out, Lou looked down the slight hill and saw a small frame house with a square dirt yard. A woman about her age in a faded blue housedress and slippers down at the back, a coffee-colored woman with fried hair tucked under at the ends, was sweeping down the yard. On the porch sat a tin watering can and at the side a rake.

"I want a chipped pork," Lou said. Then, "I'm going down there." As she half slid down the slope she could see the other woman looking at her. "I'm Lou Maxey, and excuse me, do. It's only I saw this dirt yard and I simply could not go past it, don't you know?" Lou was talking fast to cover up her nervousness and embarrassment, but she knew she couldn't go back. The woman was husky but her face was kind, with a long, full mouth. "I haven't seen a dirt yard in I don't know how long."

"I'm Lacey," the woman said, nodding toward Lou. Her voice was warm.

"Would you? I mean, this is probably going to sound crazy to you—but would you let me rake a little bit with you? I had a friend once . . ." She found herself unable to stop. "Jean Dillon— her Granny in Greensboro, North Carolina, had to have a dirt yard or go crazy."

The woman listened. A smile crimpled her cheeks; she held out the broom, walked back to get the rake.

"It's the oddest thing. Here we are—we're looking for them— the Dillons, trying to figure out where in the world they went to. And I saw this yard. How do folks lose track of things?" Lou's scratching the earth now; it is mostly weeded out and very dry. Lacey sprinkles it to keep the dust down and even, to try and set the pattern.

"Are you putting the arches here?" Lou asks, then feels compelled to explain, "One time—one time we lived together when we were young in this old crummy motel with kitchenettes and cabins," the woman nods, "with all our kids. You notice now how no one has lots of kids anymore? I had four and that was nothing to my grandma. My fifth was too far apart—like an only baby."

"I had six," says Lacey. "Six and one boy killed in the war, four girls."

"Any of them around here?"

"My youngest girl—up there. She runs the barbecue. A good girl. A fine husband. Three grandkids."

"That's nice," Lou says. "So nice to have the kids near. This time I'm telling you about—the time we made us a dirt yard. We made it from scratch. That sounds funny, doesn't it?"

"It does. It does. Usually you just clears them away."

The two women are moving shoulder to shoulder now, walking backward. Lou sweeps the dirt clear and then Lacey pulls in the design, slightly wavy lines that curve around the cement stepping-stones.

One late August day Lou and Jean sat in plastic strap chairs, fannies hitting the ground, watching the kids run dirty circles around the motel compound. Clark's Courts was marked by a line of soot-covered plaster ducks advancing on a three-legged concrete deer; his left antler was a single metal spike. Rocks, painted alternately blue and white, rimmed the swimming pool, which was choked with leaves and olive algae etched on its sides and circular stairs.

"What you need, Lou, to calm your nerves," Jean said, "is a dirt yard." Lou had had a crying jag that morning as a result of the heat and the baby pressing on her spine and peepee sheets and a

The Purchase of Order

three-year-old who bit. "My granny in Greensboro once told me she'd have gone crazy if she hadn't had her dirt yard to rake. Kids love them too." Then she yelled, "Hey kids!" They stopped their wild running to stand sweating as dirt puffed over their feet, then turned to face Jean in a band—Lou's in sunsuits and clean pinafores and roman sandals, Jean's in torn shorts and aprons tied like capes. One wore a nylon bridesmaid's hat.

"I've got a game!" Jean called. They leaped into the air, all in a bunch, mud daubers rising to cluster near the two women. Lou's timid son, tagging at the rear of the group, rested his hand on her bare shoulder. Ceil and Maisie pushed up to the front, Ceil's eyeglass frames balanced on the end of her nose, Maisie's braids fuzzy and coming undone. Autumn Ann clambered up into Jean's lap.

"Get down. It's too hot. And listen to this." Autumn Ann curled closer. Jean huddled them and Lou saw how Gordon and Jasper bent over just like Lamont, as though they had no bones but were willows being arched. "We're going to make us a dirt yard— no more mowing the lawn for us." And all those little children, some not over two years old, never having heard the words "dirt yard" before, knew exactly what she meant. You could see it in their shiny eyes as they looked around the compound to size up the destruction that could be wrought. Autumn Ann picked up a handful of pebbles and licked them. Lou was getting tickled and the baby inside her kicked out—hard. "Ouch!"

"What, Mamma? Mamma, what?" all of hers shrilled, even as their hands ached to pull up clumps of grass.

"Nothing," Lou laughed. "I guess we better start pulling."

"From here . . ." Jean stood up, unfolding her long arm like a measuring rod. "From here to that deer's broke foot, I want down to the dirt by suppertime. Now run get some things to dig with," she said.

"Can we use combs?" Gordon asked.

"Why not?" she shrugged. "Combs, spoons, sticks, anything that'll dig'll do. We need to lay this lawn bare, get it back down to the basics. Now go on and get."

Now, on this day twenty-two years later, as Lou sweats next to Lacey, using a borrowed broom, waiting for her turn at the rake, she tries to tell the story and why, whenever she is feeling low, she'll bring up that afternoon.

"There we were," she says, gesturing with the broom, bringing it down to make half-circles in the dust. "Jean in Lamont's skivvy shirt knotted at the shoulders, cut-offs, and her stringy hair plastered to her head—it must have been 95 degrees—and me, p.g. with a summer top and shorts with that hole cut in the middle for space, feeling air cool against my belly and the sweat running right across my navel, both of us hunkering in the grass, pulling weeds and clover and everything that grew. All those kids—Jean's five, my four, who knows how many others and where they came from, and everybody with a spoon, a stick, a pointed thing. Autumn Ann used the prong of her barrette to scratch the dirt back."

And every one of them, she can't explain, with a purpose, as they unearthed old bottle caps, rusty nails, cigarette butts, a pile of treasure put to one side for when the digging was done. Lou can still see clearly her son squatting, both hands dug deep into the grass, tugging at a clump, straining back on his heels to lift it by its tufted roots, pulling hard to break the sod away; can see him fall back, clod against stomach to cry out in triumph just as a grasshopper leaped free, the movement of its wings no more than the shimmer of heat.

"We did it too," she says to Lacey. "We did. By six o'clock that evening, before Marlon and Lamont got home, we had a perfect circle of dirt, so sweet smelling. Too thick to really rake, but the children went and stuck the edges with forks as if it was a big patty pie."

The Purchase of Order

"Lord, Lord." Lacey shakes her head and smiles. She's stopped raking in order to hear this story and she leans on the end of her rake, using it like a cane. How can Lou tell her of the great grass hummock to the side of the yard that got thrown and sat and climbed upon? Jasper mounted to the top of it, put a dirt clod on his head, shouted, "Lookee here! See my false hair?" then blew back dribbles of dirt that peppered his cheeks. All felt the taste of mud melting in their mouths, gritting their teeth, and the thickness of soil caking under their fingernails. As the day deepened into night the sky paled and shadowed the trees while the streetlights outside the Courts sneaked light over the wall. Then the children lay down in that cool damp dirt to push roly-poly bugs around and swim their arms and legs in those dark elements.

"Later," Lou says, "I later lost the baby I carried then, but I've never lost a second of that day." She can still feel life turning inside her as she dug her fingers knuckle-deep into the earth.

Lacey reaches out her hand and lays it on Lou's arm, and as Lou slows her sweeping, her tears spatter the dirt. "Thank you," she says. "Thank you for letting me help you with this yard." Then Lou is confused. She is standing on the edge of the intricate design and she doesn't want to spoil it. Lacey takes her arm and leads her up to the porch and over to the side. "Right here," she motions. There are three steps down to the grass. Lou sees the clothes flapping on the line and up on the hill sees Marlon leaning against a car talking to a man who must be Lacey's son-in-law. Children and a dog circle the car in a running game. Lou realizes she is still holding the broom in her hand and turns back. "Here."

"Wait," the woman says, going quickly through her belled-out screen door; it slams behind. Lou stares at the smooth dirt yard, so different from the one she remembers—this one dry and designed but still powerful enough to move her. The screen door opens again; Lacey is at the steps. "Here." She holds out a navel orange—deep russet and glowing. Lou can already taste the sweet tang of its flesh. They smile at each other, each old enough to remember when an orange was a gift you hoped for, hoped to get tucked into the toe of a stocking, or icy cold from lying on a block of ice when you were sick, sweet pulp sipped over ice chips. The color of carrots, or persimmons, of the baby Lamont cradled on his chest.

"Here's for your traveling," Lacey says and puts the orange into Lou's hand.

"Thank you. Thank you again." Lou, holding the orange tight to her chest, climbs the hill.

Sometimes on these trips, when she's tired, Lou despairs and wonders aloud to Marlon if they will ever find the Dillons. If maybe they should quit, break down and take out ads before it's too late. Maybe Jean and Lamont are dead. He always pats her on the hip, leans close to kiss between the point where her shoulder meets her neck, and says, "You know we'll find them. Now, don't give up. But we'll take out an ad if you want to. Hell, let's buy a banner. Buy a blimp. I can afford it."

She is cheered holding him and being held by him, her face mashed sideways against his shirt buttons, an errant wire of hair pushing from his neck-V. She feels his heart thrumming through her hands as she fits her palm around his shoulder blades. "I love you, honey," she mouths against his buttons. He murmurs back, rocking her in a silent dance.

Two days later Lou can still feel the broom in her hands, the scritch of the dirt, the powder of it as it moved away in patterns, and how it puffed up when Lacey sprinkled it. She fancies that if she holds her right hand cupped over her nose she can still smell the yard, smell again the end of the broomstick stuck into stiff straw, the wood split with paint flecks filling the creases in her hands. She's happy to recall that Lacey leaned on her rake, tucking the end under her breast to stand like a tripod and listen, shake her head, and smile at Lou's telling. The orange she gave her is in the cooler case at this very minute.

When she'd joined Marlon at the hill, looking back to wave, grinning until she thought her face would split, Lou felt mixed up. Once in the van, she turned to Marlon. He was looking straight ahead, left leg bent at the knee and propped up on the seat in a way that was dangerous and drove her crazy. She didn't even know how to begin to tell him what she'd done, and said, or why. She wanted him to already know it.

"That reminded me of Mamma," he said, shifting his position, making the van speed up, slow down.

I could kill you, she thought. She was nothing like that. Marlon's mother was not a thing like that. Never was.

"Reminded me too of the time ya'll dug that whole yard up," he added. Then, alarmed, "Lou, what's the matter? Lou? Why are you bawling?"

She could only shake her head. Then she lowered her face into her hands and cried while Marlon kept changing the stations, swiveling the dial to find some music to comfort her.

That night in bed at the Promo Motel, where everything was harvest gold or green shag and scarred with cigarettes, she tried to tell him what had happened to her in Lacey's yard. He held her, patting, saying, "Hmmm," or "Yeah," or "Oh, honey," gentle interruptions. "It'll be all right, sweetheart." Then he stroked her thigh in a way she always remembered. She moved to him, marveling at the wonder of knowing Marlon all these years, and so long ago, that other Marlon who'd first pulled her away from her safe home and life. She almost thought she could feel that young Marlon, so skinny, so eager, so crazy to get up and go, as he moved in her now.

A few mornings later they are driving along when Lou is alerted by the blue van ahead of them. "Catch up with them," she says. "Hurry, Marlon. That's exactly like the kind of thing they'd drive. Look at all the stickers on it."

The van is plastered with *Knotts Berry Farm* and *Save the Whales* and *Luray Caverns* and *Disneyworld* and the whole back window is covered twice, once with drawn-down green shades that filter light, then with stickers of mountain ranges and other natural wonders in this hemisphere. *Wash me! Quick!* is fingered out in the bumper dust.

Marlon, revved up by Lou's excitement, guns the motor, catches up to cruise side by side with the van. It is muraled on the side with great tongues of flame pointing to the headlights, a map of the United States with stars in every state and a tribute to the Baltimore Orioles. All the side windows are shaded in green too, and the rushing sunlight makes it seem to be traveling underwater.

"That mother's going fast," Marlon says, lowering and twisting his head to see the van off which Lou is reading signs.

"*White Sands Proving Grounds?* They never would go there, would they?"

"Hell, I don't know," Marlon says. "People change."

Lou looks at him. "This seems too new a van for them."

"Look at us, damnit," he says. "We've got a Saab at home. You think Lamont and Jean ever expected to see us in anything but an old Pontiac?" He speeds up even with the driver as Lou pokes her head up and out. The front window of the van is copper glazed with a reflective sheen.

"Speed up some more, Marlon, so I can get the angle." Then she sees, as though through fire, a young man, bearded and bespectacled, singing at the top of his lungs. Marlon pulls ahead, blinkers right, and pulls in front.

"Not them?"

"No." Lou falls back in the seat and adjusts her seat belt. "But it looks like the kind of van they'd be driving." Marlon is looking

The Purchase of Order

out the rearview mirror at the van; its great coppery windshield glints, shooting silvery lights off its convexity.

"That guy was singing with his head thrown back—singing at the top of his lungs—just like you do," Lou says, and she puts her hand on Marlon's knee.

He breaks into a tuneless but buoyant "Home, home on the range" as Lou says, "I'm gonna wave anyway. I bet there's little kids in there." She scrambles up and over to the back, undoing her seat belt and standing bent-kneed in the back seat, leans until her upper body is wedged into the back window. She begins to wag her head and wave back and forth, looking like one of those bobbing backview beagles that are so popular. In the rushing of the light made by the two vehicles, Lou's face looks back at her from the other van's copper windshield. In this strange trick of light for a moment it seems that she is sitting beside the young singing driver. She sees herself bronze, smiling, waving back at herself.

"Hold on, honey, I'm pulling out," Marlon says as he steps on the gas and moves them away.

Alice Remembers

The smiling cakes on the invitation begged Won't You Come and I delivered them, pedaling down unpaved roads, tricycle wheels scudding dust that grayed my knees and darkened the v-flaps of the envelopes. I was to be six.

This year I am thirty-three, a difficult year in a Christian culture. Jesus's example, even if you don't believe in the total him—the trilogy of Father, Son, and Holy Ghost, the last hanging like a wedding dress in a girl's closet of dreams—but only believe in the pictures of his sweet face, long hair reminding you of a virile Tiny Tim offering salvation, causes guilt. You know a boy who looked like that would be picked on. I'd take his guilt if it would help, add it to all my other: teased my sister twenty times, sassed my mother innumerable, back-talked my teachers, cheated on tests, betrayed my lover, aborted my baby, was a traitor to my country. Was I? Has self-sacrifice ever been my aim?

No, it is only the number itself causing the confusion. The 3's doubled up like that are sinister, reminding me not only of the folklore of pigs, bears, men in a tub, but the mystery of rings. Or the great fat 8 they make when they are turned to meet, snapping in a circled stack, snowmen without a head; that would terrify if I believed in the legends of the Tarot pack, the crystal, and the stars. To make a figure 8 on ice is to go back, to retrace, to carefully place your blade and cut through the center of the previous path. Done on one foot, the other is pulled up, its work over in laying your future. You must lean into the line, you must not overbalance as the chain's link meets precisely with no sign that you are taking back your past. It is a compulsory exercise that can be measured. It is stepping back into your prints to make a getaway. It is the snake swallowing itself again and again.

On that long-ago party day the Richard twins gave the invitations back, drawings tucked inside. A crayoned dog, salmon-bald patch on his back, was Chub, they said. Children stood remembering the dog who'd been shot dead that summer. Remembered the dust that puffed around his paws as he moved straight-legged down the middle of the road, shaking his square shagged head from side to side, flinging flecks of foam like a man in a too-tight collar craning his neck for water, going mad. The other picture was of a pretty girl with round blue eyes, pupils smaller than a snake's, her mouth a heart, and yellow curls spiraled to the edges of the card. My name, each letter a different color—wine, fuchsia, periwinkle blue all in layers that flaked off on my thumb—was necklaced on this waxed and papered me. I was amazed to hear Mamma say she'd frame them, hang them up for all to see, and praise those mainly dirty two as good artists and good girls. I got mad when one look-alike twisted the basket holding juice lips and penny-sized sugar babies until its handle tore. Madder still when Diane, the girl who lived in a motel, didn't wear her lace confirmation dress which I had seen shrouded in a sheet hanging on her closet door. Skewered to it was a veil drooping with net roses, like a ghost's bride. She would be married to the Lord someday, she told me. But she was at my party in plain pique. Wasn't this a special occasion?

Here is a snapshot of my sister at age two sitting on a tabletop. She is barely bigger than the birthday cake at which she claps her hands. Shoulders hunched around baby fat cheeks, sash of her smocked dress undone, she is frozen in expectancy. She has not yet blown out the birthday candles and the camera has caught their gleam; they shimmer, strange fireflies hovering above the candy roses that border the edges of her sweet. Her hairline remains the same, as though an artist penciled a delicate line around her ears, then gathered up fine hair into a tail that in this picture arches like the ink strokes in a Chinese print—it could spell *waterfall.*

When she was twenty-one she brushed her face, unblemished untanned skin, against the curve of a pot which would hold flowers or a clutch of wooden spoons. Its glaze, thick as icing laid on by a spatula, was the deep olive green of a river, and threw its tints onto her face. Under her chin the vase glowed green like neon in the rain, turned her into a girl you'd see underwater, floating downstream in a dream. Do I imagine this? Was it true? Her skin, years later, is ruddy, a husky rose, rouged and powdered; the powder clings to hair that downs the sides of her face. It is the texture of moss.

There was a birthday party for someone I didn't know, knew only, or was told, that he liked poetry; wrote poems, they said. I imagined him dark with thick fur on his arms. I imagined us in bed, his chest and back burly, a soft brown bear embracing me. He would kiss the mole on the back of my left ankle. I would comb the hairs on his plump toes with my mascara brush. We would be married, smoke Gauloise, go to Mexico or to the mountains, and wear cotton wedding shifts. I bought him Roethke wrapped in tissue as fragile and as green as fern. My inner atmosphere was hothouse lush. How can we know these things? That men write poems, might make love to us?

One by one that night the offerings spread out: Mickey Mouse ears, grass papers, a roach clip. He was not the one I thought. He tries on Groucho's nose and furry brows and grins as he pretends to cigar flick. He is rusty with yellow eyes, sallow skin. All gingery, freckled, thin, mottled, and sly. I want my book back.

He takes me to bed, saying he loves Roethke, and hurts my hips with his sharp bones. All arms and legs and vegetarian emphasis. The soles of his feet are hard and yellow and his eyes gleam in the dark like a red tomcat's. His bony fingers belie my idea of poetry, move me to passion. "Remember I met you on my birthday," he murmurs in my ear as we stand waiting for a bus, shivering in the rain, sharing an umbrella.

Will I always mourn my furry lover, my dark poet? Where is he now? Where is that book whose cover, even that birthday night, was curling from the moisture of a Coors can? Once I told my pale ginger root, whose arm hairs turn to cotton in the sun, that as a child I'd asked for a birthday gift back, a Mr. Potato Head, whose possibilities of disguise I recognized even then. Just the addition of a tie, a baseball cap, shoes that pointed in opposite directions, could change Mr. P.H. from a nothing of a spud into a creature I could love. The birthday boy had put my gift aside, paid little attention to what I knew, even then, was love—the possibility of creation, the knowledge of change. Did I really know that then? "I've got to go," I said, "let me take him until you're ready for him." My lost black swan of a phantom lover I named Foxy, hung a golden circlet no larger than a baby's ring in his earlobe, and let him lick my collarbone when deep in love. Come back, my yellow lover whispers, such waltzing is not easy.

On my husband's birthday some years ago I made a book. We have it still, folded away in a box with official documents and photographs of onetime friends whose names we can't recall. Eight pages long, each one a different color from the construction pack, yet all fading on the edges into gray, it is filled with the stick figures of our life. The first pages hold a little boy, one circle, one cross, a dowser's rod for legs. He has a happy face, and not because he is sunshine yellow but because his rocking rung feet seem to quiver, threaten movement off the page. He holds a book, five thin lines of his fingers are across its back; a title, "Look, We Have Come Through," peeks out between his bones. We ate unripened Brie, too-ripe pears, everything was off. We couldn't find any music to match our mood. I noticed my husband's ankles seemed larger. Do grown-up's feet grow? We had ice cream pie for cake; a thick twisted taper lit its center. Was that the year of a gray wool sweater thick as mail, heavy as armor, that ten years later ended up lining a basket in a Southwestern barn? Or the year of the penny jar, each one mercury-polished and gleaming fresh-minted through the glass, their copper odor gone, the promise of change in the creases of Lincoln's goatee, already going gray?

In the seventh year we'd been together we fought on my birthday. Desperately, silently, slamming into the mattress, breathing raggedly, harshly. I grabbed his ears, pulling his head like a pot of pasta; he twisted my wrists in Indian burns. "You bastard, you bitch," we hissed at each other in a house not ours. We fell to the floor in a frenzy, hoping to kill. My glasses fell off; I clawed at his nose, calling him redfaced and yellow, and coward. He whispered, "Maniac, liar, cheat." "It's my birthday, you jackass," I panted, and kicked him. Then, as I bit his wrist, I tasted the hairs on the back of his hand. We shoved away from each other, sick of each other. His nose bled steadily into the rug. "I hate you," I said. Did I? I wept. We both cried with the sun streaming in through the window, charging the air, which was filled with things invisible, suddenly seen, changing before us into late afternoon. Heavy with weeping, unable to cry anymore, we walked through the house to get ice cubes together. Kneeling, shoulders touching, we diluted the blood which had pooled in the rug's white hair. It paled to a peach that matched the sunset. Over and over we blotted, scrubbing away the evidence of love turned on itself.

The winter I was nine we lived in the small town of Sillenbuch, Germany, in a half-timbered house that was frightening. Holes beside fireplaces loomed large enough for children to burn in, rooms led to rooms that led nowhere, and all of it dark wood smelling of varnish. My mother strung the playroom with orange and black streamers and outside, in November, all the trees were bare; morning frost iced their limbs, black bones covered with grease. Hunched paper cats spat from the windows and in the center of the ceiling great smiling moons dangled in pentagrams. Yellow and elaborately pleated, showing one cynical eye, these lanterns with their flickering glow were sly as the faces carved on sundials, flat with long hooded eyes, squat gods with lap basins for blood.

My mother wore a black gypsy dress that shimmered, cut straight across her breasts and upper arms, and fell in vivid flamenco flounces to the ground. A lace mantilla tethered to a rose skimmed her shoulders, floated like a web as she filled favor baskets with candy corn. My father wore both an eye patch and a fez. I was Alice, in a Sears-ordered blue dress, glittered with silver across the hem, sparkling off on my knees leaving a gritty Gretel trail as I moved among my guests. Across my smocked yoke White Rabbit ran, his fob watch hands ticking toward my heart. "I'm late, I'm late" was written on my breast.

I've never had a birthday sung in a restaurant but I always listen carefully when someone else's is. Once in a tropical paradise, the Bali Hai, while sipping rum punch through a plastic orchid, I saw the cake first. Waitresses wrapped in flowered sarongs hipped the kitchen door open to stand in a wedge of bluish light, the glint of stainless steel, the crash of crockery behind as they lit the candles. It seemed an ancient rite, a Polynesian ritual performed by four women huddled to make fire. I waited for more but they only swayed barefoot across the room, collecting eyes to encircle the birthday girl who looked embarrassed. I'm sure I sang along.

On the day our son was born the winter turned, became freakishly warm. As I trudged up the hills of Eureka Springs, selecting Christmas gifts from tourist stores, warm winds blew down the mountains, making me sweat, causing my husband to

The Purchase of Order

push his thinning hair off his forehead, still easy to blister, temples beginning to mottle. I carried my baby high, as if he were a bay window, imagined him on all fours, peering out and marveling at this world. I wondered as I walked and chose miniature brooms, herbs in calico, if we were the natives greeting him on heartless shores, or ourselves pilgrims, fearing this strange new life we had embarked upon. He too was confused. Not due for three more weeks, he unexpectedly left his silent sea, my body the rocks to beat against. Slipping from his safe haven, red and wet with juices and with blood, our son wailed his welcome.

Now he is almost six, could have attended that first party I remember. He's the right age. Behind the Richard twins, Rob Brock stood. A big old boy in the second grade, but just a titty baby for all that, his mother said. Wets hisself every single night and most the day. He smelled, as he always did, of dried pee on sun-bleached overalls, hair wetted down but never scrubbed. He handed me a shoebox that held the best gift I have ever got: a small syrup tin in the shape of a cabin, with the door cut out and a side that folded back and forth. Inside was a horny toad which I loved more than the turquoise ring from Carlsbad Caverns or the Amosandra doll. "I like this," I said, wanting the party to be over so I could poke straws down the chimney and feed this small dragon who kept turning his head. Somewhere I hope my mother's kept that cabin so carefully cut. It sliced my fingers every time I took the toad out, and finally when he died, flat as a dried leaf, I put a small china doll in his place. It sat for years on my dresser top, yet I can't remember when I last saw that birthday present.

On this summer afternoon the cake's been cut and paper plates of it dropped in the long grass as my son plays with the birthday boy and his other guests. The four of them skirt the pond. Paul is peering through the cattails and does not see us watching. For one moment his face is turned to the sky, utterly

Alice Remembers

beautiful. They are trying to get a volleyball that has floated across to the far edge of the water. One boy is at the marshy bank ready to claim it; his determination not to share makes him careless, makes his brother reach down to grab the back of his life jacket. Paul frowns, then catches sight of us, or we compel his sight. I wave high and wide. He sticks his hand straight up in an Indian *how*, then quickly down, and looks away. Minutes later he calls us to come over. I can tell by his gingerly stepping that he doesn't want to walk on the mucky path. My husband and I are sitting together, partially shaded by an old tree. His nose is burned, his knees are red, our bare feet are side by side. The grass grows over our toes. We each call our son to come; we hail him encouragingly. "Here," we shout, then scoot apart, still holding hands.

The Christmas House

Jelly bears and Swedish fish surrounded by sugar cones, meringue rounds, and two pounds of assorted candies—nonpareils, candy canes, curls of ribbon— are on the kitchen table. Dean dips blunt scissors into hot water and snips the spearmint leaves in half. He is the only child of an only child who did not begin that way. For Dean his mother is the only connection to those who lived before. How did this come to be? she thinks, smiling and winking at her five-year-old, his cheeks bulging with sneaked sweets. How could a family that so loved the idea of family be dissolved? What had become of her imagined life as mother of three with a husband who'd dress up as Santa Claus?

Measuring vanilla into the icing, she thinks about this season. Is it one of loss or gain, giving or receiving, remembering or forgetting, rejoicing or mourning? Dying children get Christmas in July, people ache to be home that day, suicides rise and blues abound and all the magazines have articles on stress. Why, then, do I feel happy? she wonders. "Jingle Bells" begins another time on the radio on this second holiday Anne and Dean have been alone. Here, a few days before Christmas, she sits with her son, following the directions for a gingerbread castle they are building. It can always be a happy season, she thinks, if there are rituals to observe.

Years ago the three Howard children—Anne, Dean, and Carla —lived in Berlin. That was 1954, in the American zone of that divided city, after the airlift, after the war. Major Howard had been with the first Americans to move into Germany after World War II, his family safe in Ohio awaiting orders to join him. When they

The Christmas House

debarked in Bremerhaven after a stormy November voyage, he was there to meet them, his face ruddy above olive-brown wool.

"You look so good," he said again and again, hugging them, squeezing their shoulders, pinching their cheeks. "You look so good." The sight of his children, fresh-faced with straight teeth, seemed a miracle to him—he'd seen what war could do to children. Now Anne, Dean, and Carla, safe with him and their mother in Germany, were watched over by a succession of women who received in exchange a room, meals, a meager salary, Mrs. Howard's old clothes, and the Major's sympathy.

He had no judgment save pity in matters of the heart and always brought home wildly unsuitable women to help his wife clean the floors, chase after children, and cook meals. Ingeborg Pitsch, who acts as a stop in Anne's Christmas memory, came between Ursula Geike and Heidi Boehn, one fired because of wrong connections in the East, which even then was closing down, the other because she was sluttish, always having cramps and hiding pastries under her bed, an action Mrs. Howard was convinced attracted rats.

Ingeborg Pitsch and Christmas are linked for Anne in the way that blue lights tacked in a star shape might trigger memory in another person. Before the war she was a philosophy student at Frei University, sent to a labor camp for political activism, and then to a factory near Darmstadt where she made machinery and parachutes and survived. She had little family left: a brother, Klaus, in the East zone and a distant cousin who lived in Dahlem. Destitute, broken in body and spirit, she registered with the American Post Command as a translator and/or housekeeper and met Major Howard during an interview where she discussed Pushkin in Russian and was hired as an *au pair.* Ingeborg wore almost always a gray suit, once Mrs. Howard's, with the short skirt fashionable before Dior's new look, pleated blouse yellowed down the tucked lines, heavy lisle stockings that made her legs look wooden, and navy tie shoes with ribbed soles. Her homely big-boned face with its sharp nose and sunken lashless eyes was rarely still. When she raked back her hair nervously you noticed all her knuckles were too big. Her fingertips, like the skin over her cheeks, twitched as though galvanized. She'd had two mental breakdowns since the war's end, so at the Howards', while overlooking the long walled garden, she grew healthy re-learning her English against the sounds of American life as lived by the transplanted Howards of Vogelsangstrasse. Another rusty-faced woman in *putz* clothes, Frau Kleist, came three times weekly to clean and cook and fill the air with odors of cabbage and potatoes boiled too long. She left only her acrid scent behind in the bathrooms she scrubbed.

Each evening Ingeborg shyly emerged to help set the table, or hold Carla on her lap and fit the baby's hands to the keyboard and play and sing German lullabies in a soft hoarse voice. Some-times she would knock softly at twelve-year-old Anne's door, and when given admittance would stand, hands clasped earnestly in front, sneaking glances at the *Photoplay* pictures of Janet Leigh and James Dean pinned to the wall, and try to talk to Anne about the cinema.

Once she was somewhat recovered, Ingeborg returned to her studies at the university, left the Howards, and rented a room in Dahlem. She came monthly to fetch Anne for walks down Lin-denstrasse, S-Bahn rides, lunches of noodles with oxtail gravy and mineral water, and lectures on German culture, German his-tory, Schiller, Goethe, Brecht, and ballet. She never mentioned her lost family, friends, her labor, the holocaust, or her lost his-tory. She received a tutor's wage to shepherd a sullen girl, and Anne, walking beside her resentfully, thought that Ingeborg smelled like so many Germans, of heavy sweaters and suits never cleaned that exuded sweat and grease, the musty odor of clothes worn as blankets during cold nights. Anne disliked most Inge-

The Christmas House

borg's earnestness, the standing-back as she pushed Anne forward to mumble to a store clerk, "*Entschuldigung Sie mir, bitte. Wieviel kostet es?*" Then make a false purchase, lesson done. She secretly scorned Ingeborg's pride in her as a pupil, pride that flushed a circle around Inge's mouth.

Once Anne went to the East zone with Ingeborg. First riding the S-Bahn, then switching to the U-Bahn, they did not get off when they were supposed to. Both trains were lettered with the same red signs. There were announcements that said *Achtung!* Anne was excited and afraid with the feeling that although people went into the East, no one wanted to stay there. It was too cold, and poor, and everywhere were eyes. The canned goods and American cigarettes the Howards gave Ingeborg helped her keep her brother Klaus alive. Anne remembers they took him C rations left over from maneuvers, khaki cans with patties of concentrated cocoa, flat tin circles of jam.

When the last train stopped they got off, walking quickly. Anne remembers nothing about Klaus except that he wore a beige Shaker sweater that her mother had knitted for the Major, but the sleeves were too long; Klaus had the cuffs folded back. Was it a December day that she remembers as Inge's tears spotted the table, and smelling dust and emptiness in a bleak room furnished only with a cot, a table, two chairs, and a calendar bright with goose-girl scenes? The cheese they brought loosened in its wax paper, seemed to grow during the long afternoon. Anne leaned against the window, looking out at rubble, listening to Ingeborg and Klaus talking in low voices. Years later she asked her father why Klaus hadn't left the East zone. How would anyone have known if he had just walked out of his apartment, stayed on the train into the West and not swung off to wave goodbye, already turned sideways to avoid Inge's weeping, hand clutching her bangs? Why didn't he simply stay with them to debark at Kurfürstendam to ride the double-decker bus down the wide linden-lined avenue that those who didn't know Berlin before the war thought beautiful? Why not end up with his sister, safe at the Howards' house to live on the third floor and eat sour bean salad and knockwurst and do chores?

"They always knew where you were." The Major's voice spoke, thin with age. "Once you were identified, they always knew." His hand pressing the remote control made the TV images jump.

Now Anne's parents live in a pink adobe house in Tampa and Mrs. Howard endlessly washes lettuce in the kitchen. Her father remembers little of the Berlin years, or pretends not to, but he knew that Klaus had lists, knew of lists; there was something to do with Inge's brother and hidden papers, hidden lives, that trapped him in the squares of bleak rubble, the landscape of broken brick, window frames propped on concrete blocks, the refuse of war still on the ground piled in pyres that was the East. On the West side such sites existed too and the children, American and German, clambered the twisted wire rope that marked them *verboten* to balance on slabs of downed tenements.

Anne's brother Dean was five when Ingeborg lived with them. He would dart from his room to where she stood and butt his head into her stomach, bending over and hitting gut-high, boring into her like the story Anne had read of a weasel who could only get out of a sack by eating through a boy's heart.

"*Ach, ach,*" Ingeborg would laugh, patting Dean's tabled back, twisting him from side to side, dancing in a strange, slow waltz. He could speak German better than any of them and often went with her to buy the evening's bread. "*Sechs brotchen, bitte,*" he'd pipe and bring back gummy bears as treats. The first time Anne saw them for sale in an American store she wanted to protest. Tonight they are heaped on her table, stained glass shapes melting into each other.

Dean was another casualty of war. He joined the Marines after his freshman college year. A square-faced boy with small, set-apart teeth, Dean was a ball player in high school, made good grades, and never caused his family any disappointment. Major Howard was angry that Dean didn't get his application in on time and ended up at teachers' college when time ran out, but Mrs. Howard didn't mind. She liked him to come home weekends, to do his laundry. She liked to see the knickknacks shake with his bounds down the stairs. Anne had married by then, but remembers that first Christmas when Dean talked of his classes in code—Chem and Econ and Poly Sci; he was not engaged by any of them. The Christmas House that year was a log cabin constructed from chocolate cookies and whipped cream.

During the spring semester he left school, became a Marine, and left for Vietnam to fulfill the dreams of life's adventures that they hadn't known he'd harbored. His letters were written to be read aloud, so intense with romantic description it seemed he wrote with a thesaurus at hand. Writing of that lush, green, alien atmosphere, he told of "air so humid it flattens your head." Sweat beaded his stubbled hair, wet his face, pooled in his collarbones, smeared the ink of his paragraphs. "My socks are never dry, Mom," he wrote, "so I pretend I'm wading in puddles like I used to do." December 17, 1968, Dean was blasted in the chest, blown back against a tree where he sat erect with his head hanging down; he died looking at the wound that killed him. He was sent home wrapped in layers of slick greenish-black rubber, sheathed like a tree's roots, balled and burlapped, to be lowered into the earth.

The hole that waits always seems too large for the tree. How can this small live fir, thriving so nicely in a pot of bright red foil, need so much room outside? Anne thinks. It does not seem possible that it will ever grow larger than waist high. She and her son Dean have decorated it with eight ornaments: straw stars, starched string rounds. Her brother's grave was so much larger than he was. There was never the possibility of filling the hole by hand, even if each mourner, each person who loved him, had heaved shovelsful of earth, carpets of flowers. A small tanklike bulldozer waited to push flat the soil over Dean's and so many other boys' graves.

His December death ended the Christmas season for her parents, who never recovered from the shock, the knowledge that as they chose wallets, books, and socks, packed divinity and fudge, and wrapped hermit's nest cookies in tissue paper, their son was on his way to dying. After Dean's death they never bought another Advent calendar. It was too hard to pull back the paper portals that counted down the days to his death. Harder still to open the days that followed, each one leading to a last door, which when swung wide revealed the promise of the world's only son, knowing that their boy was dead.

Dean, the third, scoops frosting from a can and adds green color drops. He was named after his dead uncle; it is his grandfather's name too. After the divorce Anne took back the last name Howard that she'd grown up with and put it on again. It fit like an old letter jacket, slightly shrunken, somewhat dated, still comfortable. Dean kept his father's last name, and she hopes that this might make her former husband care. He lives in California now and sends Dean wonderful gifts—link-lock castles, talking teddy bears—elaborately wrapped and mailed from a store. Dean and Anne form miniature popcorn balls to set atop sticks of trees that dot this sugary landscape. M&M's are forced into the sticky circles to become small Christmas ornaments. Dean selects carefully, red, yellow, green, rejecting the tan, the rust, the brown.

"Save those colors for the path, Mommy," he commands. Then wheedles, "Do the grass, Mommy, do the grass next." He is impatient to get to sprinkle light green coconut shreds in a sweet snow.

Anne piles M&M's as building blocks. She thinks, as she ices the flat side of the cardboard courtyard, of what is left to do before her parents come. Turkey thawing, all the side dishes of cranberry relish and creamed onions that her mother doesn't like to fix are done. The onion dressing and the pies, pumpkin and mince, await grandmother's touch. Dean can hardly wait to see his grandfather, whose hands are rough as a dry sponge, each finger with a space between that never closes since arthritis came. Rubbing the heel of his hand on the crown of Dean's head, he makes his cowlick stand straight up.

Carla, Anne's younger sister by fourteen years, was a war casualty too. Closer to her brother in age and temperament, she was his admirer, hater, and purest friend, for in addition to being good in school and sports he was good to his little sister. After his death Carla grew quiet, then quieter, finished college, became a teacher of third grade, and continued to wear her hair held off her forehead by a tortoise barrette. A woman who wears horn-rims, jogs in a purple sweat suit from Sears, Carla still lives at home and saves her money for an annual Christmas cruise. She will be in the Bahamas dancing, Anne hopes, under the Caribbean stars wearing a dress of pink pique. Anne recalls Carla's college graduation with all the girls wearing black robes ending in red Nikes; the boys with ponytails poking out of their mortarboards. Many held signs "End the War," while others refused to stand during the national anthem.

"Carla's going to the Bahamas with a school group," Anne's mother had written, "so you and Dean had better make the Christmas House."

Carla was a baby when Ingeborg Pitsch scooted behind her on stockinged knees down the corridors in the dark old house on Vogelsangstrasse. Carla sat as center ornament in a card table on wheels with a cutout in the middle, her fat baby feet propelling it along. Ingeborg followed, inched her way, limbo-weaving on her knees, arms outstretched, murmuring, *"Liebchen, liebe, Kom-*

men sie hier, bleibt bie mir." Carla scrabbled backward, then crowed with delight as the play chair tipped, threatened to topple.

This is the first Christmas House that Anne will build from scratch, the first that Dean is really old enough to help with or appreciate. Building this one, she remembers the first. Ingeborg, then living in a small flat, invited Anne for a Christmas House celebration, a German custom the Howards hadn't heard of, and one in which Anne was not interested. She was busy memorizing the lyrics to "A Little Love" and trying to find out what teenagers in America were doing. Worse, Ingeborg had invited another girl—a German—for Anne to meet. The Major, always enthusiastic about such cultural exchanges, accepted. Mrs. Howard, rolling Anne's hair, coiling strands like snail shells, sympathized with her daughter. She also did not like the way Germans smelled. She was suspicious of them, and her fears were deeper than slogan prejudice. Everywhere the Germans lied that they hadn't known what was happening to people in the camps, the Jews, so she distrusted them, even Ingeborg. Wasn't Ingeborg's brother still in the East? Didn't that mean something? But still she laid out Anne's clothes, wanting her daughter to look nice, bring credit to her family, her country.

Ingeborg's flat was one alcove and one room, small, dark, crowded with furniture, full of the smell of food sitting out, of books imperfectly dried and now mildewed, gray fluff in their creases. There was the cloying sweetness of marzipan, the incongruity of garlic sausage exploding with grease next to bittersweet chocolate brittle across a torte, a saucer of raspberry jam nearby. Anne felt no liking for the table, too heavily laden with strange food, or for the German girl Liesl with her heavy mottled legs, thick socks, and plump breasts flattened by a dirndl. Everything that girl was, Anne did not want to be, splotch-cheeked with fuzzy French braids, alight with excitement at meeting a foreigner. Anne was aloof, a peroxided streak in her bangs, her lower lids lined with black. She nibbled the pfeffernussen, licked solemnly at the marzipan, her least favorite taste, and drank the lemonade. They talked in German, Anne's halting, then in English, Liesl's better. Ingeborg watched them intently, ticking her head from side to side, mouth twitching the words in correct pronunciation. Once she huddled them, and Anne smelled her, not rank but strong. Her nylon blouse showed that her slip strap had slipped to the vaccination hollow of her arm. She held the two girls close, pressing their cheeks hard against hers, as though they would break into trio harmony, the McGuire Sisters crooning "*Liebe, liebe.*"

The raspberry torte was dry, crunching to dust, the pudding thin, cheesed with gelatinous strands. The room grew hotter, close with doggy wafts from the German girls' wet wool socks. Noises from another room or the flat next door grew louder and Anne's head ached. Liesl never stopped smiling, cheeks staining redder, eyes glowing as night came. Ingeborg switched on a lamp, throwing over it a printed scarf that shadowed the room with leaves. Music swelled from the radio as she lit the Christmas House. Ringed around its icing yard were twisted silver trees with candles in their centers. The candles too were twisted spirals of white. One by one they sprung to flame, illuminating the candy house that she had built for them, all gingerbread ormolu, windows of melted sugar, spun thin, rolled flat, a roof rickracked with thick paste dripping down in icicles: a perfect chalet of patience and desire. The two girls ooh'ed and ah'ed. Anne couldn't help it. It was too beautiful to maintain her armored poise. They leaned to look, pushing their hands back and forth as if they would touch it. Ingeborg looked anxiously at them.

"*Der kuchen ist sehr schön,*" Anne praised.

"Is bootiful," said Liesel.

"Ah, good," said Ingeborg. "I am much pleased. *Sehr gut.* Now eat." She waved her hand as if to say, "Let the feast begin."

Both girls shook their heads no, oh no, they couldn't, how

could they eat such a beautiful thing? It must be left, to be saved, to be seen, to be enjoyed.

Impatiently Ingeborg shook her head, said, "To eat, it is to eat. For this I made it. To see you, for you to see, then eat it."

Even as they protested again, she snapped off a shard of ice smelling of almonds and pressed it into Anne's hand, then broke off the door and lifted it to Liesl's lips. "Please, *bitte, alles essen, bitte,*" she begged. "To eat—*esse zusammen* for me."

They stood shyly, eating tiny bits, plucking up a golden gatelock coin, a candy cane marking an eave, as Ingeborg, tilting her head from side to side, moving her jaws in encouraging chewing motions, watched them eat the beautiful Christmas House. As they ate, growing greedy, the girls began to giggle, sputtering pieces of cake, and Ingeborg was pleased, smiled widely, embraced them, happy at this breaking-down of barriers.

The last hour of that night was an exercise of smiles and blushes, crumbs spilled and liquid spilled, and parcels wrapped to take home; the exchange of addresses became embraces and the exchange of affections. Anne was bundled into her coat as Ingeborg tenderly wound a muffler around her neck. Liesl helped Anne with her gloves. Then they walked her to the bus stop, holding hands unselfconsciously, and snow softly fell, hazing the streetlamps, dimming the bus lights as it charged through the mists. Anne leaned across a seat to wave at the two standing under the light, their shoulders covering up with snow, bulky as epaulets.

Telling her family about the evening, handing Dean the present wrapped in tissue paper printed with pines, he asking "What is it? What's in it?" her parents wanting to know who was there, how it was, Anne to her horror and embarrassment burst into tears. She didn't know why she couldn't explain it. So she did not protest her mother's explanation of too long a day, too much strain being with people unlike oneself all day. Even as she sobbed against her father's chest, she knew her mother's reasons were wrong. Dean ate the icing off a roof's edge and Carla ate a marzipan fruit which turned her lips orange.

The next year, back in the States, in a suburban Virginia high school, Anne was elected cheerleader, cut her hair shorter with bangs, and was told she looked like Molly Bee. That December, Major Howard brought home a Christmas House and thus began the Howard tradition of having a different house each year in a different style. That one was from the NCO Wives' Bake Sale.

"It looks like a quonset hut. Nothing like Ingeborg's," complained Anne.

"You decorate them, right?" asked her father. "Soldiers need Christmas Houses too."

Her mother made khaki icing and outlined the windows with silver dragées. "Your dad was in the Army Air Force, but never got to fly. And never got over his love for hangars, kid."

Dean set an Army helicopter model right in front of the house. He'd made a little sign: Rudolph the Red-Nosed Copter.

The year that Dean died in Vietnam they'd started the house right after Thanksgiving so he'd have a photograph of it finished. It was called "Snow Covered Lodge," its frosted roof thick with white pebbles of nonpareils.

Here in this kitchen Anne Howard and her son Dean are finally ready. All the castle parts are made, cooled, laid out along the plans; they must only be assembled. Dean holds up the first walls, their glued edges of icing stick and clinch. The third threatens to cave in. With the fourth it becomes a bungalow of hard brown bread. They're both intense and sticky. The table is littered with knives, spoons, spatulas, every implement to be used for decoration.

"Look, Mommy." Dean holds out a hand webbed with spun sugar, fingers encased in a sticky net. "I'm a duck."

She reaches for him, first licking her own fingers, then cleaning his hands with kissing licks.

"Leave some for me," he says. He solemnly sucks his two middle fingers as he did for comfort as a baby, then moves his mouth back and forth as though playing a harmonica as he eats icing off his wrist. "What do we do when it's done?" he asks.

"We look at it, admire it, say how did we do it—then after everyone's seen it we eat it."

"Eat it?" His voice is incredulous.

"That's the best part."

"We eat it," he says with a giggle.

"Gobble, gobble," she says, making him laugh.

This Christmas Castle was hard to put together, hardly the simple project, the easy evening Anne had thought and the magazine directions promised. Walls fell in, candies slid down icing to plop in the yard and get lost in the frosting drifts, tree cones toppled and died. Assembling a house took a touch she didn't seem to have. Her fingers stuck, pulled things apart even as the edges tried to hold. Finally, as she and Dean carefully, so carefully, cement the roof in place, she remembers Ingeborg's hands with their huge bruised-looking knuckles. In repose her hands were always cupped, the skin trembling with involuntary commands to fist up and protect the hidden lifeline in the palm. Ingeborg's hand looms up, candle lit. That glorious Christmas bungalow that she had built and then urged its destruction is somehow here on this table. And the two girls—so different— gingerbread pilling their lips, laughing as they crunched the open doors of Ingeborg's offering, are grown with their own children.

"Let me tell you a story, Dean."

"You're sure that we eat it?" Dean asks again.

"Absolutely," Anne says, "or what did we do it for?"

Bow Wow and Good-bye

No one *ever* said "insane." They said "madder than a hatter," "crazy as a coot," "nuttier than a fruitcake," "off their rocker." Somebody needed to be in "the loony bin," "the nut house," "the cracked shack." Or they'd twirl a finger alongside their heads and say "a gear's loose," "a spring's slipped," or stick out their tongues and gasp "gaa-gaa." But I'd never heard them say "insane" or "emotionally disturbed" or "mentally ill." Things for them had not changed from Bedlam days. They even liked the sound of "bedlam" that night I tried to move their minds, enlighten them.

"She shore talks good," said an aunt.

"I could listen to that girl all night," yawned an uncle.

The word "bedlam" rolled silently on their tongues as they imagined poor old crazy things tied up to walls, eating with their hands.

"It's a crying shame," Grandma said.

"Shore is," agreed my aunt, pulling a long pitying mouth over her bucked and lipsticked teeth; this caused her mascaraed lashes to stick out like wires. "You wouldn't get me near 'em!"

Yet in Lawn, their small Texas town, there lived a madman who each day whirled his way down Main Street, pausing for a breath and a short plié in front of Hart's Drugstore before he circled off again. There was no joy in this spiraling like a child's windmill; at least he never smiled, only every now and then soberly stroked his hair as he chain-turned his never-ending rounds. "Poor old Carole Partin," people said if they thought of it, but mostly they didn't. He was, for them, as regular and as natural as the tumbleweeds turning lazily in the dusty roads.

The Purchase of Order

The word "mad" was reserved for Grandpa puffed up, turning red as a Crayola. If the boys escaped a beating, they'd gather in the back bedroom with its three sagging iron beds, uncurtained shades askew, to whisper, "Whooee, is he ever mad!" then shake their butch-cropped heads at their good luck.

Nor did they ever use the word "crazy," except for one uncle who insisted on nicknames, "Flash," or "Spats," changing them as often as he changed his shirts. He'd burned longhorns on his arm with a red hot coat-hanger brand one football season, and once, emulating Alexander King on late-night TV, he bought hot pink socks. Sluicing his face at the kitchen sink, he'd shake his head like the old dog Frisk and mouth "Crazee" when asked to do a chore. He planned to play the clarinet in a jazz band and run away to Mineral Wells, maybe Dallas, and blow that licorice stick until he forgot the smell of oil fields and the feel of greasy dirt gumming underneath his nails. The word "crazy" belonged to him. Or sometimes it was used for old people who lived alone in shacks. They walked the miles to town, slashing at the highway with long sticks, muttering to themselves. "Poor ole crazy Sister Hawkins," folks would say, and everyone agreed that the isolated elderly were not in their right minds; might even eat canned cat food or never cut their toenails.

"Berserk" was a word that made them scrooch down in their chairs and giggle, a word somehow too fancy, too la-di-da, only suitable for scary movies when doctors in white coats said in haughty British tones, "My dear chap, this fellow is berserk!" and caused the doctor's friend to come all shaky-looking. Once at the Holiness church a visiting missionary showed movies of the African village where he lived. Close-ups of dark faces covered thicker with flies than pies set out to cool, and the talk he gave after, his voice cracking as he talked of good and evil forces, made folks uncomfortable, sent the women scurrying to the church kitchen to put out angel food and the pineapple-upside-down cake. Of him Grandma said: "Well, he's a good man but berserker over that village to my mind." That word was right for him.

"Losing my mind," Grandma said a hundred times a day, claiming that "ever time a nickel is laid down around here, I hardly get my pockets inside out and that money's gone; I'd think I'm losing my mind, except ya'll been buying Woolsworth's out these days."

But then Great-aunt Wilma decided to go insane. She had a checkered history anyway. There's one like her in every family. She'd married once or twice—the first time eloping with a sergeant sent to sign up boys who thought that breathing in mustard gas might be no worse than mucking in manure. He'd set up a table with a sign behind "Uncle Sam Wants You," and that pointed pinky reeled them in like nylon line. When he packed his duffel bag and recruitment lists of country boys who'd soon be buckling their puttee straps, Aunt Wil went along. Even then she'd had her dreams: planned to act, to sing, to eat chow mein, ride the Staten Island ferry, have lovers (and she said that out loud), write poems, stories, songs and plays. "I never even saw a letter sent all that time she was away," complained Grandpa.

Here are other things she was said to have done: joined the WACS and wore a uniform, or maybe served coffee in a Red Cross canteen; took tickets at a movie house in Chinatown, got a tattoo on her spine, "a small quite lovely butterfly," and once fit children's shoes, where she learned tricks to flatten out fat baby arches so high-topped leathers or rubber boots could be pulled easily on. She was a park ranger, or a fire watcher, a poll taker, something that required a clipboard and an official manner— she could discuss statistics, charts, and graphs. Somewhere she learned to sing scales and she do-re-me-ed down sidewalks, quite oblivious to stares of men in cowboy boots and pushed-back straw hats, who cared nothing for her sweet trills but watched the pushing up, the independent pulling down, of her square rear end.

For years Wilma'd lived in a two-bedroom frame house on an unpaved street; lived there along with her piano, her Peace roses, and her collections that nieces and nephews were allowed to handle under her sharp eye. The girls danced the Dresden figurines around, the boys juggled the Jivaro head. She made lemonade from scratch and a chicken salad that was legend because of its miniscule dice. No one knew exactly how she got her money to live. Her second husband had been known, but briefly. During his sojourn of a few months he mainly slept, bought crackers, cheese, and bulk bologna from Hank's Grocery where he greeted folks' "hello's" with a strange sideways nodding of his head. But that was years ago.

Now Wilma announced that she was tired. Tired of plunking out rhymes and rhythms alone, worrying about the meaning of her dreams, her future: she was ready to cave in. She'd made her decision, she said, during a trip to Austin when, after viewing the capitol, the museum, dinosaur footprints, and the university, they'd driven slowly through the grounds of the state mental hospital. It was quiet and cool and green, and all the people walking around had looked peaceful. She didn't believe the women were patients at first, until Grandpa pointed out that their hair was mainly cropped short and their dresses blue cotton-striped.

"You know," Wilma said once home, "I thought they looked real happy. Not laughing or fooling around, but walking peaceably, and sitting and thinking in the shade of all those trees. That food smelt pretty good to me, too," she added.

"Wilma's always been crazier'n a kite from the first time I laid eyes on her," Grandpa said. "Treated that last husband like a damn dog. Made him sleep out on a rollaway bed on the side porch. Said he disturbed her thoughts. Finally she chased him right on outta there—his own home. No telling where that poor guy is."

Bow Wow and Good-bye

"Well," answered Grandma, "he wasn't a grand prize—shrimpiest man I ever saw. Big old bug eyes and a loose mealy mouth. Why Wilma ever took up with him is beyond my means. She was a nice-looking girl, with dimples *that* deep." Grandma's thumb flashed in a measurement for the depth of dents in cheeks. "Not what you'd ever call pretty—too feisty for that—but real handsome."

"Humph." Grandpa hawked his throat clear. "Always mooning around in fringy shawls and painting roses everywhere you didn't want one—that was Wilma young. She was lucky to get that pip-squeak."

"And luckier to get rid of him!" Grandma countered. "Whatever you say, and you can say a lot about Wil, she's always had her own mind. She makes it up to do something, that girl does it!"

What Wilma had made up her mind to do was to lose it. Toward this end she moved with a stubbornness "that proves that everything I ever said about that crazy woman is true," said Grandpa. She checked out psychology texts and talked of aberrations with the same passion once given to the picking out of tunes. Her poems dealt now with "therapies and sociopaths," and all her dreams seemed to be of flames, or stealthy walls moving in, turning into fingers of the dead that jerked the sheets off her toes.

"I swore before, I'd sooner pay ten coyotes to howl than have to hear Wilma sing another song about love of ivy vines and men who left her low," Grandpa grumbled. "They wouldn't have left if she'd ever kept her mouth closed. But now, I don't know . . . I don't relish these new songs about axes beating in heads and blood-drinking by a midnight moon."

"Oh shush," scolded Grandma. "Some of Wil's new songs have a lilt to them." She hummed one that started "Lone Star, you are my own star" and ended with the sun breaking into bits like shattered peanut brittle.

"This proves it though, doesn't it?" I said. "That she really is insane? I mean, look at all this running around to study what kind of crazy she's going to be!" I was triumphant, home from my first faraway travels. I saw this as Wilma's life-choice, an exciting event; one could be anything one tried, but especially not yourself.

"Don't surprise me at all if she really is crazy," Grandpa said. "That woman's got a mind like a rusty steel trap. It just snaps shut, then festers."

"You hush now." Grandma defended her sister. "Wilma's always liked the new, liked to know things. This will keep her occupied." Always on the edge of her sister's knowings, Grandma thrilled to the risks Wilma took, the dangers she'd dared. She'd always trusted that there was basic common sense to stop Wil from the step that caused the cliff to crumble, her body to follow.

That year the tales of Wilma were relayed by mail; kin as far away as Lubbock heard the news. "My Dear Kids," Grandma wrote, "Sunday dinner before church your Aunt Wilma came over and liked to scare me to death! Snuck into the living room and sat in Grandpa's La-Z-Boy, quiet as could be. I heard a noise and thought the cat had choked on a hairball, so flickered on the light and there sits Wil! Big as you please, she opens her mouth and screeches. Well, did I ever get mad—wanted to take off my moccasin and give her a lick, she staring at me bold as a hawk. I says to her, 'Wilma Gene Jones, what in the world do you think you're doing, sitting up here on the Lord's day, in the dark, screaming at me?' Honey, she moves all fidgety, looks like she's fixing to sing, so I says, 'I want some answers, girl.'"

The answer was that Wilma, having done research, was now embarked on field experience. She thought a scream or two in the dark might move her faster into the ranks of those with minds half gone.

"But," Grandma wrote, "she couldn't do it right, is what she said. She never was one for screaming scared, or screaming of any kind, for that matter." Then, reminded no doubt by Grandpa

of the shrieks that'd run Wilma's pop-eyed spouse from home,
she added, "But that other kind of screeching was different—
more yelling like, flanging around and working up a sweat, getting over a fit. But sitting with her feet up on a hassock and
shouting out at me. That wasn't like a looney, but a fool."

A few months later Wilma cut her hair. Waist-length, thick as
mink, with silver strands coarse as steel threads, it was her one
real beauty. Every night she bent over at the waist to throw it like
a cataract to her knees and brush one hundred strokes; the hair
tips moved as though alive in the pulling of the brush.

"My Dearest Kiddoes," Grandma wrote, "Wilma whacked her
hair off and it looks like an idiot put a bowl on her head and
hacked at it in the dark. Told me she chopped it with pinking
shears! Now she won't get it trimmed right or styled or wear a
wiglet or nothing. Looks so messy, falling ever-which-way because it's always been so wiry."

Unleashed at last from its anchor of braided bun, groping
wildly after years of stability for something more substantial
than ears to cling to, the hair was Wilma's first real sacrifice.

"She buried it too," Grandma wrote. "I tell you it was scary. She
took an old stuffed panda, tied that hank of hair around its neck,
packed it up in a shoe box, dug a hole near the pecan tree, and
laid it in." She'd sat on the porch swing until dark, slowly cant-
ing her new light head from shoulder to shoulder. Later she took
no notice of a niece's offer to pierce her ears using an ice cube
and a wide-end needle. "It wouldn't hurt a bit, Aunt Wil," the
niece begged. "The worst you'd feel is the dripping of cold water
on your neck, I promise." The girl's voice was breathless with
desire to pierce pure gobbets of flesh, now so freshly pink, so
vulnerable. Wilma "phtted" through her thin lips and, testing
her lobes with a fingernail, leaving half-moons, said, "Nope,
thanks."

She took it slow and easy for a time after the hair episode, letting her family get used to the idea, having made up her mind that it wouldn't do to force others to her way of thinking all at once. Always a collector, now she began to gather lengths of string, and rolled them into balls, first orange, then grapefruit-sized, and finally huge knobby gray rounds that could be lobbed from a foul line. She fed all the stray cats she could entice into her yard, and for a summer tried to get birds to land on her. Standing still and crooked as a scarecrow, peanut butter dabbed on outstretched hands, she finally gave this up because she kept getting dust flecks in her eyes and bird plop on her head. She collected shopping bags, stuffing them into each other like onion skins, and she carried this rustling hobo sack everywhere she went, hanging from her elbow with two purses: one red patent, the other raffia with lots of starfish and shells woven in.

"Keeps herself clean," wrote Grandma, "and that's all I ask. Doesn't pull at her clothes, or dig her nails into her cheeks, or let herself get smelly. Wilma's just like she always was, only more so."

At the Fourth of July reunion, family laughter was uneasy. Relatives hunched over the redwood picnic tables, holding down the tablecloth against the wind, and talked of Wilma.

"Hung her hair up in that tree before she buried it. Sat and swang on her swing and stared at it all day," Grandma reported. "Said it was like watching herself be lynched." Aunts and uncles and assorted kin sat silently. Some wagged drumsticks in the air; others used their index fingers to clean their plates, waiting for a cue. "Don't that sound like . . ." Grandma hesitated. "I mean, maybe she has . . . maybe she's . . ."

"Gone and did it!" interrupted Grandpa. He finished his iced tea, then crushed the paper cup. His eyes, narrowed and troubled, were dark as two raisins in a pudding. "Said she would, and by God, did."

"The Lord's name, shame," said Grandma. "She's in that recluse state." Then laughed. "You'd think we was professors the

Bow Wow and Good-bye

way we know it all. I swear I don't know why we repeat it either because the one we're getting it from don't want to know her head from a hole in the ground."

Aunt Wilma shorn was thinner, her face aged like a student made into an oldster for the high school play. She spoke vaguely past me, never meeting my eyes; often she talked to pictures of the dead, glassed-in face up, on her coffee table.

"All those people where you live . . ." She shook her wispy hair, pressed her fingers on the glass tabletop, leaving prints. "I don't see how you do it . . . all those people. I saw in *Life* where everybody was walking right in front of cars, didn't even look at the traffic lights. Nobody paying any mind to anybody else . . ."

"Sometimes," I said, "sometimes it's easier to live with a lot of people who don't know you—who leave you alone."

"Yes, maybe . . . maybe it is. That place in Austin was so green. I never saw so many trees. You could smell the grass, just cut, clips of it were on the sidewalk. All cool under the trees and that grass cut just so. Everything so quiet." She paused. "Everybody seemed so calm, so good-natured."

The next time I visited she told me about a story she'd heard. An old woman had killed herself and left a note pinned to her blouse. It was a note to Prince, her pet spitz. "I can't go on," it said. "Bow wow and good-bye." Aunt Wilma shook her head, sighed, then said, "You know, I couldn't blame her a bit. Frisk's been better to me than any man. Flops down when I'm feeling low and licks my hand and gets all sad-eyed with me, but let me lift one finger like I'm going to play 'My Buddy,' he's up and wagging his tail like a fool." Frisk, a pudgy piebald mutt, lifted his nose, then lolled his muzzle from side to side as though asking if Wilma would play or not. We both laughed.

"But that's too sad," I said. "Think, Aunt Wilma, to have only a dog to say good-bye to when you die."

She shook her head. "No, it's not. Not nearly so sad as not having a living nothing to bark at. Sometimes I could howl for lone-someness. March right out onto my porch, throw open my throat, and howl!" With that, she screamed a loud head-thrown-back, neck-cords-cinching-up, a screeching, howling, ulalating hoo-ooo-ooo-ing that faded into a softly crisp yip-yip-yip, ending with a breathy ki-yeee. During it all my aunt was centered in her chair, her back straight, hands clasped, knees together, and an-kles touching, her pink Dearfoam slippers pointing outward. I charted the howl through her, saw it pulse over the knob of her wrist, watched it lift her rib cage up and out, and saw it beat in the vein that bulged in the back of her heel. That glorious call halted in her big left toe; it twitched, swelled, seemed to purple with the pump of oxygen. She whoofed out the last of her air, settled back to say, "Yes, my girl. Arf-arf and fare-thee-well—I'd say *that* said it all." She let me stroke her hand.

Not long after that, when I was gone back to city life, she began the "heebie-jeebies" with a soft "ha-ha" at Sunday supper.

"Ha-ha what, Wilma?" asked Grandpa.

As if looking at him made her not want to laugh anymore, Wilma pushed her plate back, scornfully watched him make a hole in his mashed potatoes so he could pour the gravy in.

"Just 'ha-ha' is all," she said tartly, then frowned, remember-ing it wouldn't do to get angry if she was supposed to be glad. She took a mouthful of beans, glared at him, and muttered, "Hee hee."

"Wilma, you'd better share your fun before you strangle up," said Grandma, passing plates of green tomatoes and okra fried in meal.

Wilma had planned a laugh a bite, but laughing and chewing are not at all compatible, so supper went on in silence. Soft sounds of mastication, gulp swallows of tea, clink of crockery; the sound of celery was riotous in their ears. During dessert of banana pudding, when each soft slide of pudding seemed to push their eardrums out, they'd caught each other's eyes and started to laugh.

"Kids," wrote Grandma, "Ya'll a died. There we was—three fat old folks laughing to bust ourselves. My good Sunday platter fell to the floor, and Frisk snapped up a piece of chicken fried steak and *that* liked to tickle us to death. We laughed so hard that darn dog dropped the meat out of his jaw, and Grandpa fell to the floor and acted like he'd gobble it up. Then Wilma was laughing, practicing like a maniac, going up and down the music scales, saying she couldn't stop laughing, don't make me laugh anymore. I laughed till I cried. We was gonna watch TV, but Grandpa said it better not be no funny show, and we got tickled again. Oh, it was really fun."

I pictured them, heads knocking beside their plates, nose to nose with china rims, hysterical tears wetting linen to wood, their hands stretched out, touching: a seance with laughter as the medium, Frisk's tail-thuds the tapping from the veil beyond; the banana pudding congealing on the table, ectoplasm turning gray.

Laughing stopped when Aunt Wilma found catatonia, for with this one she'd found her niche, slipped into it like sliding into a satin quilt.

Grandma wrote, "Wil's new one means she don't talk any, don't hardly move, so we can't find out a dadblamed thing. But, kids, it surely worries me because she's letting her house go. She sits in that old blue chenille robe and stares at her toes. You know that's not like her."

Grandpa was at first uneasy, then grew angry. "That damn woman! She thinks we got nothing better to do than try and poke something down her throat. She's starting to smell like a dead armadillo."

"She's sick is all," Grandma defended.

"Made herself sick," he said.

"That may be so, but it's up to us to take care until she gets this out of her system. There's lots more she hadn't tried, waiting in those library books."

But Wilma tried no more. There was no need to. She sat quietly in her house, daily growing dirtier. She paid no mind to folks' fingers scratching at her door, to the hungry cats that wound around the posts of her back porch. Margarine tubs filled with leavings grew green in the icebox, shopping bags remained un-stuffed, lights either on or off stayed that way, and day by day she continued to sit, her hair now jaw-length, lank, falling like wet twisted twine. She'd chosen a brown recliner to roost in, but she'd not stretched back. Wil'd wedged in the corner, one hip balanced on the chair's arm, the heels of both hands pressing the ends of the armrests, readying herself, it seemed, for a dive, so tightly were her fingers held, so perfectly poised for a jackknife's salute.

How she maintained the pose was a marvel. Her knees curled up, her slippered feet neatly crossed at the ankle, it seemed there was no place she was supported but was held there by her desire; flash-frozen in the act of getting up or sitting down, relaxed or afraid. Her fingers revealed her rush to flight, her knees her giving in.

"Oh, Wilma, Wil, Wil," Grandma murmured, stroking her sis-ter's thick, oily skin. Dirt gathered in the impress above Wilma's lip.

"I wanted her to buck it off like you'd do when something tick-les underneath your nose," Grandma wrote, but Wilma would not. They called in a doctor who, after one look, bundled Wilma up and sent her to Wichita Falls, where her body was built back again. Tubes carrying medicine and vitamins ran into her arms and nose; one disappeared beneath the sheet. Her case was diag-nosed as a classic. "Every symptom in the book," they said.

"They took Wilma to the state hospital yesterday," Grandma wrote. "It felt so strange driving behind the ambulance, seeing bluebonnets out on the highway and not hearing her yell 'Stop!' because she'd got to get out and think up a song. She'd always tramp around in them, getting Grandpa mad. Used to make up a song a trip."

Wilma's songs were family jokes. The best, "Bluebonnet Eyes," is about a blossom pining for a brindled poodle who'd stopped for a run along a stretch of purpled field.

"Wilma was miked out in a navy silk and her good shoes, and kids . . . she wet on herself. We didn't know about that until we stopped for co-cola and gas and the attendant told us. He said Wil started to shiver in the air-conditioner so she was blanketed up. Poor little old thing, she's about the worst I ever saw, but like Grandpa says, she brought it on herself."

At the Holiness church everyone prayed to get the real Wilma back, and much was said to Jesus about the sins of stubbornness and stuck-up ways and reading books, yet finally, though no one really could understand, they cared.

"Everyone here has been good to her, giving little things to take along. Sister Wells made a crochet bag in the prettiest pink for Wil to keep soap and Jergens in. She fixed little roses fluffing round the top. Grandpa like to cried when he saw that. You know Wilma always was the one for a rose of any kind."

Her abandoned side porch, an arbored white lattice trellis, was overrun with roses. Lush Glorys, British Beautys bent bushes with their weight. Fleshy petals littered the flat surfaces in her house, dry-dripped from the jelly jars she'd last stuck them in, glass bottoms now a tangle of scum and leaves.

So Wilma was gone. Her yard grew up, weeds covering the walk, and people borrowed pressure cookers and cheese graters from her kitchen, rasps and rakes from the garage, and forgot to return them. The front porch overhang developed a leak, and a bedroom window screen pulled out and screeched in a high wind.

Relatives kept close eyes on the young ones coming up, and

when a niece played her own made-up composition on the violin, Crockett High auditorium was dense with kin watching to see what the angle of her head or the graceful gliding of a bow could foretell. Or, if not that, to try and fathom why *this* gawky girl, skinny calves wobbling in her first high heels, could think up such a thing. How unlike Wilma she was. The youthful Wilma was pert and plump, her knees set off like shiny pearls between flapper hems and circles of rolled hose. Her dimples stretched her mouth in every photograph. How had she, so popular, so lively, so much fun in the early promise of the hugging-in-of-life, gone so far away? They all clapped too long and too loud for the singsong melody. The niece stood stoop-shouldered, in maroon rayon, blushing with the flush of public praise. *She* would be famous, live in big cities, travel to Rome.

Home for the summer, I was caught up on Wilma. "I haven't been for the last two months since this blood sugar thing," said Grandma, but others had been and the visit made them feel real low.

"Just sits there," said one aunt. "Just sitting there. I'd go outta my mind." Then she giggled self-consciously and rolled her eyes up back under her lids. "Wilma doesn't do nothing. She don't blink, wink, itch, scratch, blow her nose, or shift an inch. Simply sits there *all day* holding onto that smelly bag. Why, Wilma don't even move when flies get on her, and I'll say that's good control. I shooed 'em off her once, and tried to get her to talk, but it's like talking to Charlie McCarthy without Edgar Bergen." Everyone laughed as she craned her head in jerks like a marionette.

The doctors were no help either, were snobs who wouldn't answer simple questions like "When's Wilma coming round and coming home?" My aunt lowered her voice. "It doesn't look good. Doesn't look like Wil's ever gonna get well. Looks like she plain don't want to. Gonna be content to sit out her days down there in that old room. Wears the same clothes every day. And it smells exactly like pee!"

I could not imagine it, how or where she sat. I could only see Wilma that one night, poised on her front porch, face canted to the moon, telling me a story about loneliness through a loud and circling cry.

So, because Grandma could not go, there was nothing for it but I should. It was a trip I would have made with or without their knowing. The hospital buildings in Austin were faded pink brick, nestled in long sweeps of olive-colored grass which was always being mowed. The clippings catcher blew green dust across the narrow walks that crisscrossed everywhere. Huge brass-bound doors were hard to push open, but once I was inside, the walls were pale blue and gray and welcoming. High up in arched central corridors oak fans paddled cool air around. The doctors, nurses, and the various counselors—all hot, wrinkled, and harried—tried to be helpful, but they were not encouraging.

"Little we can do," they said, and "Perhaps someday new medication," and "If someone could break through." I laughed, once, then sobered as I saw their shocked faces, sizing me up. It's genetic, you know. Could I be a link, tell them something they didn't know? "I'm sorry. Excuse me . . . It's not funny, I know that. It's just that my Aunt Wilma is known for . . . she's *famous for* making up her mind and never changing it. If she wants to keep us out of it, she will." I hoped, then, for a nod of recognition of what I saw in her, an acknowledgment of the Wilma I knew, the one with a life different from this one they supervised.

I was taken to the dayroom where Wilma sat her days away. A chunky attendant said, "She's no trouble at all. Soils herself now and then if we don't get her on the pot, but I don't think she likes it. Some of 'em like it—but I don't think she does." She tucked a switch of hair back into her netted hair roll. "We feed her good, she eats real nice, though she's not one for heavy chewing, and then she goes to sleep. Mostly she sits or sleeps. She likes that chair she's sitting in." Then added, "I think she does."

We three were alone in a long room filled with leatherette sofas and steel tables and yellow wooden straight chairs. The natural light was intense, even with makeshift sheet-shades tacked across the windows. Aunt Wilma sat in a slat-back chair with curving arms, one hand on an armrest, the other in her lap, a grimy pink bag looped over a lax wrist. Her hair was very short and totally gray. Her scalp showed through near her temples. She wore a blue cotton dress that snapped up the front. Wil's left leg was drawn under her; the other dangled down in that classic pose of children in studio portraits. The attendant pulled me up a chair, then whispered, "She don't have no panties on because we're trying to make it easier to keep her clean," and looked anxiously to see if I minded.

"I understand." Then I scooted that chair so I was knee-to-knee with Wilma and put my hand on her fist. "Hey . . . Wil . . . Willie . . . Aunt Wilma—it's me." There was no answer. I thought I had expected none.

My aunt's eyes concentrated on a square of white sky, shadowed by tree limbs seen through one wired window. I stayed about an hour, talking quietly, occasionally telling a story or a joke I knew she would enjoy, sometimes hummed old songs. But I was really busy studying Wilma, looking at the earlobes that had never been pierced, the brows that would never be plucked again into those high arches of surprise, thin black lines of disdain, a doll's delight. I put a Mars bar, a lemon-scented soap and a package of wintergreen Life Savers into her bag, then tucked the raveled edges of the roses beneath her hand again.

"In-sane," Grandma finally had christened Wilma, stressing the "in" as if at last the word was exactly right to describe Wilma's latest whim. She was, they believed still, putting them on. Inside herself sane, but hiding out until she felt like giving up the game, was ready to snap out of it, write up a punchy poem, compose a catchy tune, admit the joke, and become again their wild old Wilma, that dizzy dame, who'd never had the sense the good God gave her.

I leaned to kiss my aunt and breathed in the smell of unwashed flesh and unconcern, that old odor of age which is both wet and dry, skin flaking off fingers and spittle circles caught in the corner of a mouth. "Good-bye now, bye-bye, sweet thing." I leaned over, looking for a long time at my aunt, wondering why I wanted tears to be in her eyes that never moved from the window to my face, so like hers, it was said—"high flaring nostrils and eyes showing white all around." Had I really expected that she wouldn't answer me? Who'd heard her coyote call, that one glorious release that moved from the back hairs of her neck to the ends of her big toe?

I felt a terrible pressure in and on my chest, and in my throat a fist doubled up, pushed underneath my chin, forced my head back like a plate, or a head on a plate. It was a cough, a bark, a growl, all moving up through me like a visible column. I stood still to let it have its way. Now I remember tears and snot and wet running over my chin, but I can't remember sound. Only painful releases of breath. What I think people who learn to speak through holes in their throat feel the first time they try to say, "Hello, I am fine." In their gusts of breath all grief explodes for the loss of words and the trying to tell of it.

Houdini's Wife

Bobby tries to push you away. He's been doing it all his life. When he was growing up in Brownsville, Texas, he rigged a tightrope out in the backyard, a piece of manila rope, frayed and prickly, strung taut as he could get it between the metal Y of the clothespoles, and about three feet off the ground. When his mother, Leilani Thomas, came out to make him get off, he crouched down and feinted her away with a broom handle held for balance.

"Go way, git!" he shouted, sweat plastering his bangs. "Git. Leave me alone to try this here."

Leilani, I can see her now, backed away in tiny half-steps, shaking her jaw-length hair, and watched her only boy, nine years old, scrawny, face as shrunk by doubts as a little old man's, toes clutched on hemp, swaying against a flat blue sky. He wouldn't move one inch until he heard the screen door slam.

He's told me about that walk. The thrill that filled him when he pushed to a stand and felt the rope hammock-rock under his heels. "Oh, you can't think what it was like, Sue, feeling it sag and shake—and I walked it."

Leilani's told me her version too. How she'd sneaked out the front, circled the garage, and stood behind the avocado tree to watch Bobby—Clay McGee Thomas then—rise up in a single confident motion; as the line drooped down, he was suspended in a jump roper's pose before he began his ascent, conquering the slack as he challenged the hill. "I would not have believed anyone could have done it—not even Houdini," Leilani told me, "and there's Bobby moving step after step crossing it. I could hardly stand to look at his face, he was so determined."

Houdini's Wife

I mark that walk as an important point in the development of whatever it is in Bobby that makes him like he is: cutting through clear air on a rope half the size of his boy's wrist, trying to get to the other side. It's exactly like Bobby to choose the thing to test all his skills—of balance, strength, direction, and fortitude (rough rope gives you splinters)—and, of course, some task that most would fail.

Now this: twenty-one years later, he's heading for trouble again.

"You can't do it, Bobby," I tell him. "They'll get after you. You might get fired." I think again. "No, you *will* get fired." I'm watching him adjust red feather earrings I bought at a garage sale.

I'm not exactly sure of Bobby's plan, but I do know, and say out loud, "This is another good way to make people avoid you, Bobby. A real good way. Push them out at arm's distance and sock them with your pocketbook. No, my pocketbook," I correct.

"Sue . . ." He leans closer to the mirror, examining his nose, which he pats tenderly. "This idea came to me. It makes sense. I thought it through." He bends to smooth his tights. "It's a statement I have to make."

Exactly what that statement is is what I want to know. I could almost admire Bobby in these duds, even if he didn't have a philosophy about them. Bobby has on a plaid challis skirt in plum tones, a ribbed sweater a bit short in the wrists, navy tights, and the largest pair of low-heeled pumps I ever saw in my life.

"Where'd you get those gunboats?" was my first reaction when he dumped his purchases on the bed.

"St. Vincent's—size 13DDDDD."

I didn't even know they made women's sizes that large, although with kids growing taller every day I shouldn't be surprised. Then it struck me, seeing tumbled on the bed a lacy tangle of slips and teddies and negligees you only wear on your honeymoon, and sweaters and blouses and two or three skirts.

The Purchase of Order

"Bobby, what's this all for?" Because I'm light and little, though hard as a rock, none of this stuff would fit me. Besides, purple is not my color.

"For me," he said, stripping down to his nethers, balancing on one long, large, and hairy leg to slip on a rosy satin slipper. Propped on the end board of the bed, Bobby's foot, satin-shod, looked like a bad dream where, if you're a girl, your breasts sprout fur, or like a wooden fist ripping through a lacy prom glove—strange, unsettling. I looked away and wished I hadn't stopped smoking.

"I'm gonna try all these on, Sue," he warned. All I could do was nod and let my mouth go watery, swallowing and swallowing as I watched Bobby—my lover, spouse, and friend these last ten years—don matronly clothes about a decade out of style. He slithered into a large black slip that really needed a foundation garment under it. I realized I was tightening my butt and saying "Clench, release, grip, release" silently as Bobby hemmed around in his slip, mules swirling the bottom a bit as he got the feel of flare.

I interrupted with a cough. "Well, Bobby, I got to fix dinner, so come on down when you're done."

He canted his head toward me and his counterculture curls, cropped short, framed his face. Bobby's had a pirate's circlet in his ear for years. Now his hazel eyes were a million miles away, deep into a scheme he'd hatched to push people away from him and then blame them for his trouble. "A man's gotta do what a man's got to do," he said in a challenging tone.

Suddenly I was also aware that he was wearing what women are always taught men want to see you in or out of: lacy under-things that let your breasts peep through, a whirl of satin that skims smooth legs, and frippery feminine shoes that allow only a shuffling trot—all silky material that moves under men's hands, slips over and off of flesh, cool on their palms, delicately piled on the floor. I'm wearing Levi's, a V-neck T-shirt, and Dr. Scholl's sandals. They flip-flop too, but because they've got wooden soles you could grab one and rap it smartly on the temple of anyone who was bothersome.

"Dinner soon," I said once more, sternly, and out of the corner of my eye saw Bobby holding up a blouse I wouldn't be caught dead in.

Later, while he was doing up his things on the fragile cycle, I called Leilani.

"Yoo hoo." She always Indian-love-call answers.

"Lani, it's me. Bobby's at it again."

There is a long pause while she adjusts the shoulder rest and clamps the phone to her ear.

"Yoo hoo," she says again. Leilani is drawn to phones in novelty shapes, in this case a pair of big red lips—cute, but they can barely whisper sweet nothings.

"Can you hear me?"

"Yes," she whistles, "yes," she shrieks.

"Lani, he's got a new scheme, but this is one that will definitely get him fired: dressing up in women's clothes!"

She makes no sound. I've been at Leilani's enough to know that she's spraying off her counter as she skirts around with a red lower lip clung to her ear.

"Women's clothes!" I repeat more urgently and real loud.

"Why?"

"Who knows why? A new philosophy. Something someone said. A new trend."

"I saw on Donahue that men carry purses now . . ."

"But they don't wear skirts."

"They do," she instructs me. "Leather ones in New York City."

"With their wife's feather earrings?"

"I wouldn't know about such things." I can tell Leilani is already stretching away from long distance, yearning to go in and see "Hill Street Blues."

"Do you have any idea of what we can do about this?" I don't want to beg, but I thought that after Bobby and I left the Click commune he'd put costumes away for good.

Lani deftly overlooks the *we*, slips it back to my side. "That wire act was the beginning," she says as always for a token comfort. "I don't know, honey. Try and keep him out of trouble."

I know I can't, or shouldn't, count on Leilani. Every time she visits or we go there it's evident that she's older, skinnier, and more tanned. When she dies, Lani will look like a trimmed-down stick floating on the river. Besides, Bobby's mine now; that's one reason she was so glad we finally got married. Everybody beaming in my folks' living room on the day we exchanged vows—all smiling, but me and Bobby. Me because it was obvious all I had to worry about, Bobby because he couldn't figure out how to say "yes" and make it sound "no." He finally settled on "I guess I will," which provided him an out.

Lani's been gabbing while I took a wander, but as I listen again she's only telling me what happened last night on the Bob Newhart Show.

"Honey," I break in, "I've got to go. I'll call you when this business is over."

"It will be, doll," she reassures. Lani's always had the greatest confidence in me, especially considering that the first time we met I was wrapped up in the aqua novice robes of the Click-tight, the level of silence, aqua meaning the blue of underwater where there is no speech or sound, but only bubbles of air pushing past. There were things that pulled me to the Clicks. The same things that made Bobby be there and made us recognize each other. The dial tone begins buzzing and I hear Bobby putting away his new clothes.

In bed with Bobby—after he loved me sweetly and spontaneously, then spoiled it by saying he knew I'd question his manhood if he didn't—he lay eager and waiting to hear me deny I had had that thought. "Damned either way," I murmured, and he heard "Damn you," so felt gratified. I said aloud, "Please tell me one thing, Bobby—tell me what it was that triggered this new direction in clothes?" I sounded like an interviewer at a fall fashion fair. Bobby has the most beautiful body. I had my cheek against his broad furry chest and felt his voice reverberate like a walking bass.

"Everybody's always talking queer this, queer that, homos, gay freaks, butt boys, all that stuff. After a while I got tired of it. I got mad," he said.

Bobby works in a downtown center, a School in the Streets, doing construction when the grant money runs low. I don't see the kinds of things he does, not anymore—all the sad old poor, all the bunged-up kids, everyone he and his organization try to save. I answer phones and type labels for the Triple A office, and show nothing of myself but what I want them to know. Bobby suffers every day.

I know that he's been teased or stung or picked up on a look that may or may not have been meant for him, overheard a wisp of conversation. From one phrase ("I don't know—it's good theatre") Bobby once built a revenge drama to rival Shakespeare. Bobby doesn't have it in him to shrug anything off. I didn't used to either. That's what brought us together.

He's turned now, wrapped his arm around the pillow, leg across the sheet, deep breathing and radiating a heat so high we'll never have to get electric blankets. He's left me feeling lapped, nuzzled, hugged, and heavy with satisfied love, and he's so innocent he thinks I'm sleeping too. Sometimes I think we are like the rope line and the buoy, one bobbing, the other trolling the endless current of the sea. Who ever knows what makes people fall in love, helps them recognize whatever could bail them out of life's loneliness? What is it that pairs up, often with unerring grace, two unlikelies who will get along? That never means it's easy either. From the first time I loved Bobby in bed, I knew I was dying to get up and go.

He was in the Clicks before I was. I was in the street dropping in and out with friends I'd made the day before. All names like Sunbeam or the 12 O'Clock Express, half of them as confused and scared as I was, the other half not. When I'd call home, not wanting to be back there, not wanting that room with a white twin set covered in peppermint striped spreads, I wanted something. I talked a grand adventure while Daddy tried to find out where he could send a fifty-dollar bill.

Leilani's told me she used to go by bus to where she thought Bobby was. No matter what I was doing, hokeypokey with three-year-olds at a day care center or assembling a Blimpie, I was always that Indian girl in *Broken Arrow*. I was always waiting for my love to come and hoping it wouldn't end like the movie did.

Who knows what it was that caused me to want to become so free and floating, to leave my safe circle and my life and strike off to find something, along with all the other millions who were wandering around in buses painted with flowers and flames? What was it that drove us to think to plant potatoes and grub them up when we'd never watered an ivy at home? Was it the sense that people our age were finding out things, and just the things we needed to know—all those odd yearnings we didn't share except now and then with a friend who'd look at us odd when we said them? In high school I wrote a note in study hall to a friend and said I wanted a man with the legs of a mastodon to embrace me—not really knowing what such a wrap might entail or if mastodon was the same as masculine. I remember well her reaction. She handed it back to me, all folded prim and tiny as a spitwad, and said, "You're sick." I believed her.

So here I was on a street in a drizzle that threatened to pour and saw ahead a group of people of all ages looking both jolly and spiritual in their various colored robes, shining like dinner candles in a box. I wanted to be with them in general and one in particular who as he stood—hair to his shoulders, big white square teeth smiling and a long robe falling to the ground over what could only be called a classic tailback's body—made me know I'd found where I should be. I fell for Bobby hard, and for the Clicks because he was with them.

"Why are you named the same as that song?" I'd asked after that first time in bed when I fell back with such sweet surprise and gratitude for this boy who was my every dream come true. Under that magenta robe he wore Levi's, a rolled sleeve T-shirt, and regular jockey shorts just like my brothers.

"If your middle name's McGee, you couldn't be anything else. Besides, it's my theme song." Right there on the sleeping bag pallet we were to share for a few months more, while we stayed on with the Clicks, he began to sing those "nah nah nah nahs."

And the night that we decided we didn't need the group anymore, but had found in each other what we hoped they'd provide, was at another outdoor do. We were high on something (that was almost always the case) but whether it was red, yellow, or bright blue pills, maybe only each other and the knowing that we were in a special kind of love—that night served to push us along a new way. Our mouths met wide on each other like megaphones. "Nah nah nah nah," we sang into each other. Breath followed words over our back teeth, lilting sounds drying out our tonsils as we giggled through the song, our eardrums bursting with our own sound. In that drizzle (it seemed to rain the whole time with the Clicks, our robes were always flapping damp on the hems), the bonfire smoking behind us, Bobby and I spun like Sufis; toes pressing together, we made a column of sound. Tighter and tighter we held as our Click capes swirled around us. "Nah nah nah nah," we choked out in a laughing maniacal way, while the other Clicksters clapped and ho-hooed their support.

How happy we were! Bobby recognized in me, and I in him, that amidst that group and in all the world we each had a slice of sanity. Between us we felt, as we whirled in the rain, that we might make one-half of a person to go on.

The Purchase of Order

Whatever it was, it held and has helped us through all the moves and the changing of jobs and the things that Bobby can't cope with or understand and the hardness that I see happening in myself, but over and over it is there. We thought to run away from convention and marriage and all the trappings that seemed death, and yet we married. We set up our houses, such as they were, with the matching-up of toothbrush holders and bathroom rugs, like everybody else. We didn't want kids, never did, yet when one came we found ourselves watching Pampers commercials with care.

When we lost our baby we learned another thing too. I lay in the hospital bed, my arm bundled to a board, and heard the doctor tell us how lucky we were to have got there in time, that tubal pregnancies could be fatal. It seemed to me there was nothing in the world I wanted so much as this baby we hadn't wanted and now would not have. All I could think of, swollen and sorry for myself, was of all the wrong and mean and bad things I ever did to myself and to others. And how sorry I was that I did them. How much I wished I hadn't. Even thinking if only somehow I could make it different, though I knew such wishing doesn't help. Bobby sat, his jeans patched with a tapestry rose on one knee and the other embroidered with his sign of an archer, arrow pointing to his shin. The denim darkened with my tears. I couldn't stand to look at him because I knew he was thinking of all the things he'd whispered to me that he'd got caught in and regretted. When I tilted my head to snuffle, I saw him looking straight at me with such a tender sad expression that I burst into loud sobs.

"I'm sorry," I cried. "I'm sorry."

Bobby is the only person in the world who knew all that I'd done and hid. I was the only one who knew most of what he'd hoped. "I'm sorry," I said again and again, while Bobby stroked my hand and said, "I'm here."

Houdini's Wife

In the beginning, when I was still agitating over when Bobby and I would be married, we went home. I was brought up odd but respectable and I knew my daddy's jokes about POSSLQS masked a real worry. My dad loves Bobby, who was a known element in one sense, a Texas boy too big for a compact car, too small to play college ball, and he was right at home helping boys like Bobby learn a trade when they were at loose ends.

"At least Bobby got through high school, got his degree," he said. You'd think Daddy would cap and tassel him at the dinner table. He could hardly keep from tweaking Bobby's curls. "Kids I work with can hardly ever get through."

Bobby would raise his head and his upper lip in a sickly grin, say, "Sir," and ask for seconds.

"Don't-think-they-don't-know-we're-doing-it-Bobby" was one of our very worst fights, early in our relationship. I'd said something sweet and insinuating about the trip down to my folks' ranchette when, to my amazement, Bobby turned red, flush seeping up from his net crop-top to stain his neck and ears. He shook his head at me, "No," like a cow twitches off flies.

That night with us both in Grandma's old bed, which creaked when you shifted and twanged when you tried to be still, my parents in the upstairs hall, I trailed my fingers along Bobby's chest and whispered, "I didn't know you could blush, Mr. McGee." Then I was stupefied when he scrinched the springs in a flip to his side, up on his elbow, schoolmarming me with his finger.

"You should be ashamed" was the gist of his rude conversation. "Letting hints drop about our sexual lives." He could hardly say "sex" out loud. He was over me, haranguing, his breath hoarse and harsh. "We're not even married," he said, "what about that?"

Then I was so embarrassed, burning inside, that Bobby, who I thought never gave a stick for convention, should care, should feel ashamed, should want me to feel ashamed, that I felt sick, felt my cheeks heating up, and felt a fever begin in me hot enough to light up the bed. He went on about duty and home and obeying thy parents as though he hadn't slammed the receiver down in Leilani's ear a few days ago or stomped around his sister Coy's apartment in Houston over a mere question about the future of our relationship. Now here he was giving me a lecture that turned me from hot to cold and back again. A lecture that I'd recognize later as Bobby McGee's best of the push-away form: make you deny me, he'd be saying to himself, make you betray me, expose me, go away; I work better by myself than anyone can. But then I didn't know any of that. I was twenty-two years old in my grandmother's bed in my parents' house with a man who was supposed to be my lover and my best friend, but who instead had changed, was saying the meanest sentiments, meaner than those I said to myself, all those things inside I'd never cared to examine. I stood up in bed, springs stretching down like a sprung-out guitar, and stepped to the floor.

"Get out. Get out of this bed," I ordered in a Jesse James tone. "Get out and get down on this rug." Bobby fairly scrambled in his eagerness to be kicked and chastised.

"Lay here," I said. Then in one swift move I swarmed over him, mouthing him, stripping and straddling him, riding him until I had to cover his mouth to stifle his groans.

"So there," I muttered. "This is it."

But Bobby still moved under me, his sweaty back making a soft popping noise on that wide plank floor, the rug shuffling under his thighs. He rocked his head "no, no" and clasped me closer. I lay on him full length, melting down, and felt him tighten, and twitch to stay inside. All our slippery loose connections made us seem like African talking drums. I tried to adjust, handholding on Bobby's shoulders, but he grasped me by my hips and hissed, "Stay here." At least I think he did. I heard the exhale of *ssss* and the inhale of *hhh* and I was content to interpret that in the widest way possible. Lying there wet, and smelling the wax from the floor polish, I knew what we had. Oh, way before all our losses and our years, I knew that guilt and grief, with all their sorrows and surprises, were givens in our love.

On the day of his working debut as a semi-Christine Jorgensen, I'm on tethers waiting to see what Bobby will choose to wear and wondering when I should expect to hear from the emergency room if he gets razzed. He looks like a candidate to teach Business Skills: dark suit, white blouse, a conservative gold chain, and unobtrusive pumps and hose. I'm relieved since some of the Mae West outfits he'd modeled for me lately had me in fits. Even Bobby had to accept that those would be fuel to a flame.

"Wish me luck," he says and pecks my cheek. He's clean shaven and smells of bay rum.

"Of course. Have a good day." My Bobby McGee, my Houdini in his changes, is off to face the world in his own way. There's something in Bobby that won't allow him to let life be easy for himself, or for anyone. When he fears it becoming so, he jabs it awake, even if he has to wear a girdle while he's doing it.

I worry and worry all day but don't get any calls so think it must be going all right and, to my surprise, it is. Bobby bursts in, blouse out of his waistband and all grins, not minding the run in his hose the way I would.

"Well, they sat up and took notice, that's one thing for sure," he tells me. "Perked everybody up. Made them shut up. Made them think about all that's said that we ignore. Made them . . ." This is Bobby on his soapbox, a stage I've come to know too. But his passions are always grounded in the good, whether it's soybean milk and miso, or now, making people see that clothes and who wears them and why are hardly worth the battle we put up with wire hangers for.

"I'm still trying to formulate my ideas on how folks look at you and what do they see and think about," he says.

"Well, honey, you're really giving them a lot to think about."

"Yeah." Bobby grins. "I am." He goes on to tell me the reactions of Howard Burkman, a cretin in his office who had been moved by Bobby's appeal to stop and talk about why he still says "queer." He stretches over and grabs my hand. "You're not still mad, are you, Sue?"

I thought about it. When I thought I *was* mad at Bobby, when I slammed around the house screaming, "Bastard shithead," was I mad? When did his every action, no matter how bizarre, become another unfolding of the package of Bobby McGee that had been there all along, whether in the robes of the Clicks, a white shirt crossing a tightrope, or now in this knife-pleated skirt. Bobby was still a person I wanted to get to know.

"No, honey, I'm not mad." Then his expression becomes so like a Bobby of one steamy summer that I ask him to slide over so we can kiss a little.

A Teller's Tale

I was good at that miming from the nose up, keeping my chin still and never pursing my mouth or licking my tongue across my lips. I practiced lifting my brows until they ached, but felt the pain worthwhile when a quizzical rise, right-timed, would cause Aunt Lillian, who was dying, to cross her eyes in pleasure, clap her hands, and write "Ha! Ha!" in bold letters on paper scraps. It seemed she was dying for years in a cancer ward in Wichita Falls, but time has never been my strong point. It is always too fast or too slow—with me limping down the middle, missing buses, or having to read all the *Reader's Digests* in the waiting room.

My aunt was nipped away bit by bit, and near the end she could not speak. To hide the agony of flesh she wore a mask—taped onto her ears and settled into the collar of her robe; the smile on that painted face seemed both sad and simpering, like the molded lips of a buckram Snow White mask on sale at Halloween. Her eyes were heavy browed, and she moved them in eloquent arches as she scribbled notes on square white pads. It was too late, she felt, to learn to move her fingers like the deaf. As I read her words, she'd tilt her head, watching my eyes carefully to see exactly where I was, reaching out to grasp, to pull attention to an especially witty bit. Sometimes she'd roll her eyes in gooney circles to indicate just what was meant.

Now she is dead and my legacy is photographs. All are faded brown and many are wrinkled, foxed with age. Some are nibbled at the edges, gummed with black as though a baby in the house had tasted them after eating licorice. It is natural that I be the one to have these, for it is assumed that as a single woman I have no need for china plates or extra sheets. Those were given out to married nieces years ago. Aunt Lillian and I were thought to share a need to house our kin as in living Shinto shrines. We were seen as the keepers of a family grail that the married others—with families growing, going on wienie roasts and college years abroad—were too busy to care about, except when they are having a family tree commissioned for the den. Unwed women come in handy then, they think without any cruelty. We were both librarians, so in their minds our nights are dull without cards and catalogues. Or else they think we know the mysteries of the alphabet, and how to label in white italic print each memory of the past. Not a role to be slighted, yet I wanted more. I wanted to tell—to be the teller of the tales, not just the bookkeeper who tallies the accounts. Both these were my Aunt Lillian's privilege—both the facts and the knowing how the facts will go. But my mother now moves into the speaker's place, for she has the necessary flair to tell dramatic stories over peach cobbler and hand-cranked ice cream.

She doesn't like to be compared to my late aunt who, though sweet, was very plain. Not even the animation of Lillian's face, the folding into smiles, saved her from homeliness as they save the heroines in gothic romances. My mother is a beauty from the Baptist side: she would be unhappy if she felt her nose grow like Pinocchio's into the shape of Lillian's.

We have all been looking at the pictures on this holiday eve, and soft brown paper faces are passed around: Uncle Delbert's sweetness remarked on, Uncle Panama's funny name, the twins in their perfect imaging. Here in this square are two little girls sitting side by side on an antimacassared chair. Perhaps six years old, with horsey faces framed by ringlets drooping from a center part like beagles' ears, these twins were ninety-three when I saw them last. Great-aunt Eve had the whiter hair, rinsed with vinegar to keep the yellow out. Pictured in the past, these four bright eyes—glazed with tears or just a change in chemicals—stare toward a hump hidden under a black drape. The shape of a shoulder shadows the edge. An era is captured in this shared face.

"Here is how it all began," my mother begins. One day or night, in the dim of dawn or the scarlet of sunset, twins were born. The tale is that they were born together, right on time, as if in the womb they had decided on a fixed routine. On hearing this I pull my eyebrows up and down in disbelief, like Lillian or Groucho Marx. An infant Yin and Yang, their features puzzle parts, a chosen Siamese stance; it will not do.

"It's true!" my mother defends indignantly. Her flushed face might come from heat whirring from the opened oven door.

"I didn't say it wasn't," sulks my sister, who is always quick to take offense, as if she liked to feel left out, maligned; now she'll push at pie crust, pick at congealed peach halves, until my mother pats her absentmindedly. Then she'll smile, a tiny one quirking up a corner of her mouth: the smile of a baby when it has gas, or when you lay a finger near its lip.

The twins were as like as any two of anything can be. "Peas in a pod," Mother says. "Two prune pits" was the phrase of my late aunt, though why this choice I never knew, unless the darkness of the flesh around a plum held for her a deeper mystery. I suppose my child, if ever there is one, will say "A Xerox copy." This time Mother offers a new and stranger one: "As like as two fried eggs." It fits somehow, an image of a great white circle filling up the frying pan, the yolks two cozy suns staring straight from the center.

The twins' first years aren't clear, the facts are few. They were born and their mother died bringing them into the world, and they grew up in Schenectady, New York. That name itself is myth in this bleak and barren part of Texas, for it is the sound of cold and snow and immigrants and teeming life and foreign-ness.

They were too . . . Here there is always a pause, a getting up for coffee, a rustling of clothes, sometimes a peering out a window. This restlessness doesn't subside until it's said that they were *Catholic*. Before a recent marriage in our clan, my mother claimed she'd never met a papist. My granny from the beauty-Baptist-side still claims she hasn't. She sees the new relative's Sunday Mass as just another funny thing to do, like making jewelry cases out of cigar boxes and topping them with curls of macaroni sprayed gold. But once the word *Catholic* is said, there's a sigh of relief: now there's a real reason for all the strange things those two did. In my dreams, the twins move through years, scapulars thumping softly against flat chests and bony backs, rosary beads plump as berries girding their waists.

One twin studied music and became a pianist—grand, of course. Carnegie Hall was where she played. "When," I ask, "was that?"

I am answered with shocked looks and veiled hostility from those who think that I am above myself.

"Well, I don't really know." This from an older aunt who doesn't tell stories well. Her voice fades in and out, and she too often veers to prayer, forgetting what she's about; but she is, by virtue of her age, a reference work. "A right long while ago," she wavers. This answer satisfies everyone but me, but I don't persist. To press on with questions means fixing the sleeping pallets on the porch.

Great-grandma married while her twin, the musical one, remained alone, but not for long. The spouse—clearly a villain—was always referred to as just "him" (said with a sore-tooth puckering) and was described only as a "fuddy-duddy of a businessman." My mother says "fuddy-duddy" in a slow and nasty way, as if it were a word for perverted anal acts. Once "he" was characterized as a "scallion," and even though I knew he would have been gobbled up in omelettes, the word seemed right in this

wrong state. Calling "him" a *rap*scallion might have made him
into a man intent on things like "sexual congress."

And it was sex that caused the marital split, for Great-
grandma had the hardest birth that she and her twin had ever
seen. Funny how climate must affect those things. Years later in
Texas she bore eight children, gardening until her water burst,
then fixing biscuits after she and the newborn were bathed. I will
bear my babies in Sonora, drinking tequila in the heat until my
pangs begin.

The baby was an angel child, delivered at first cry into the sly
womanish hands of the Pope, busy in Rome tallying infants who
would in the future send jewels, give tithes of 10 percent, perhaps buy toothpicks made from slivers of the cross. These sentiments had, of course, never been expressed by the twins. Rumor
had it that sometimes there was incense in Great-grandma's
room, or else she and her sister talked in Latin together so children couldn't understand. But it was the prospect of more births
and this poking in the dark that made Great-grandma swell, not
to mention that it left her twin out, that made them make their
move: they would run away.

"Sold their jewels," Mother says, eyes squinched against her
cigarette. "And their seed pearls too!" For years I thought seed
pearls were something more, delicate kernels, pure and refined,
each one worth its weight in freedom.

From flight to when they settled down, little is known save that
it was hard. Great-grandma cooked, Great-aunt played piano in
saloons and gave lessons, and together, in hiding, they moved
across America, finally stopping in Erie, Pennsylvania. Erie-ites
thought the father was dead, but those two rarely thought of him
at all, believing that he would be too occupied in "fussing with
his business" to hunt them down. Forty years earlier he might
have been a blackbirder, but in the era when they ran, there was
not the sin of slavery to blame on him. I have decided he will run

The Purchase of Order

a sweat shop and I plan to fill *my* tale with the Triangle Fire and starched-bosomed girls, hair flying from pompadours, leaping to death from seven-story tenements.

Late one night in the small house where they lived—one sister softly playing chords, one making tea or rocking her child—he is there, and not alone. With him are five, ten, perhaps a dozen men, all in leather boots and holding guns. Here is where Aunt Lillian narrowed her eyes, lowered her brows, and said in a harsh voice I once thought dramatic, but now know was cancer, "And they were fierce!" My mother does the same; I fear those husky cells.

Once my aunt made them Klansmen, sheets flying in the night, the holes in hooded heads as frightening as stars in negative. I remember questioning her, for "he" was a Catholic, after all, and I always thought the Klan went after those too. "Well a'course they do," she snapped. "That Klan, as one well knows, goes right after everyone." She hurried on and never put it in again. I will, if I can figure out the way.

Let's say he is coming. After four years on the trail of wounded birds, he is finally closing in. The Klan has met in a large saloon and he enters.

"Gimme a whisky, straight and large," he orders.

"You from 'round here," asks the Klan leader, adding stupidly, "stranger?"

He explains, and watches the men's necks bulge big in their collars, eyes sparking with the excitement of a chase—if not one kind of slave, another that would do as well.

"Let's go get her, men!" he shouts, and in one great roiling mass of men, horses, and sheets they set off.

What he did was bad enough, whether accompanied or alone, for he broke into their twinned peace, pulled the gut strings out of the piano, and smashed my great-grandma with his foot, or cane, or whip. Then he snatched up the nightgowned child, her baby hair rolled up in rags, and rode away.

A Teller's Tale

When I was little, Great-grandma would brush her hair, throwing it over to make a tent I could climb inside. I felt safe in that dark cave. Her feet planted wide, body bent, she was still but for the faint tugging of her strokes. As if peering from a waterfall, I'd part the strands around my face to see, in the mirror, my reflection, Godiva-draped. She'd carefully save the strands pulled from her brush, rolling them into ringlets that she'd put into a candy dish on her dresser or give to me to paste on bald baby dolls.

But that night she grabbed for his boot, his stirrup—then leapt and clung to his pommel, straining with one arm for the little girl who screamed with a terror that stayed with Great-grandma forever. Later, when a Texas child would cry, the twins always ran, panicked and clumsy in their ankle boots, to find pinched fingers or splinters in a toe. He burned the house too, but when he set the fire, or how, never matters next to the vision of him rearing high on horseback, the baby girl held like a sacrifice to winds, as he slashed at Great-grandma and she clung to his saddle.

"She begged him. Lord, she did. Said she'd do anything, go anywhere. Even said she'd stay with him and leave Aunt Eve." There is shocked silence; we shake our heads, look down at crumbs on the plastic tablecloth. "But he wasn't having none of it. Just kicked her in the head and rode away. She laid in the dirt, the house behind her all afire, and Aunt Eve stood between them, wringing her hands in her apron front." There is silence for a while as we each imagine the scene. Sometimes the child is given words, but even when she is not, her drawn-out wail circles the room. My sister smiles her small quirked smile. She's always liked fires; the promise of arson hangs in the air.

Great-grandma went a little mad, and always was a little different after that. Her twin took charge, moved them into a boarding house, played piano, mopped floors, cooked meals, and came home nights to brush her sister's hair one hundred strokes. Finally Great-aunt moved them to Oklahoma, met there a sweet soft-spoken preacher's son, and showed him to her half-mad twin in hopes that it would do. It did, and he took both of them to Texas.

When my mother, their youngest, was not yet born but fated, this story ended. It was a Sunday after church, dinner laid out with all the littlest children in the kitchen drinking iced tea out of jelly jars, when there was a knock at the front door.

"Go see," Great-aunt yelled to the oldest boy. Standing there was a woman in a cloche hat, a red silk dress, and T-strap shoes. According to this boy, now a navy man retired, only her nose showed.

"Yes'm?" he said. He was always polite, and he always tells us so, even now when we see two peach-cobbler spots shining like buttons on his shirt.

"Will you tell your mother that Miss Erie's come to call." He left her standing on the stoop, and on his way back to the kitchen let it drop: "A Miz Erie's right outside."

Great-aunt stopped eating, her knife and fork held in the air like metal wands. My great-grandma closed her eyes and nodded once, just once.

"You mean that's all?" My sister's only heard this story once before; she naturally wants more. She will someday tell that Great-grandma toppled from her chair, smashing into the dining-table leg and bringing the dinner down over everyone. Actually, that's another story, of Mamma giving birth to me. She lay moaning as the room filled with curses and advice. "I remember," she always tells, "feeling wet all over—gravy in my hair, waters at my heels." Now she answers, "What do you expect? For her to jump right up in front of all her other kids and say 'My darling baby daughter's home'? Why, they didn't even know she'd had her."

"Grandpa did, didn't he?" My sister is persistent. She wants to get the story straight, or as straight as she wants it for her own purposes.

"For heaven's sake, I suppose he did." My mother is impatient to finish now—whether or not Grandpa ever knew is not her myth. In mine, he will not know. He will try, on this clear Sunday, to figure out what it all means. Between the liftings of fork and food to his mouth he will stare at this woman with whom he has lived for almost twenty years, who will not look at him now as she passes plates deftly toward his end.

Miss Erie came in, of course, and stayed to sup. She listened to piano playing of hymns and finally stayed to sleep, sharing the bed with Patsy, who always peed in it and who did that night. The next day she left, never really to come again. She married a Catholic businessman and was rich, for she had a fox stole for her shoulders, two little redheads snapping at each other near her neck. She sent her mother and aunt ten dollars each on every holiday.

At ninety-two the twins drove to Arizona in a pickup truck, taking turns shifting gears. At ninety-three they died. Great-grandma had a stomach pain late one night, cuddled up to her sister, and in the morning was dead. "I'm lonesome now," Great-auntie said, and by afternoon, head resting on her lost twin's pillow, she no longer lived. They were buried together, of course, and Miss Erie came. Swathed in black, a veil draped to her knees, she read her beads like braille and moaned through yards of black gauze net. "She really carried on," my mother says, sadly shaking her head. "Just think . . . remembering all those years." Aunt Lillian used to say. "Cry . . . did that woman ever cry! I never heard anything like it."

I have not decided how to end this tale, for usually it is told that Miss Erie stayed to eat funeral meats of coconut layer cake and fried chicken wings, and in the afternoon she'd even laughed. At eight that night she was driven to the base at Mineral Wells where a plane flew her back East, her veil folded into a handbag square. She never came again but sent an annual greeting card.

The Purchase of Order

I cannot reconcile this end. Someday I will tell that she stood swaying in the heat that shimmered off the grass and began to howl a deep sad sound that stole the air. Then she threw herself into the grave, high-heel pumps tattooing grief on the twin coffin-tops, and had to be forcibly wrenched away a final time.

Previous winners of
**THE FLANNERY O'CONNOR AWARD
FOR SHORT FICTION**

David Walton, *Evening Out*
Leigh Allison Wilson, *From the Bottom Up*
Sandra Thompson, *Close-Ups*
Susan Neville, *The Invention of Flight*
Mary Hood, *How Far She Went*
Francois Camoin, *Why Men Are Afraid of Women*
Molly Giles, *Rough Translations*
Daniel Curley, *Living with Snakes*
Peter Meinke, *The Piano Tuner*
Tony Ardizzone, *The Evening News*
Salvatore La Puma, *The Boys of Bensonhurst*
Melissa Pritchard, *Spirit Seizures*
Philip F. Deaver, *Silent Retreats*